MOB TIES 6

Lock Down Publications and Ca$h
Presents
MOB TIES 6
A Novel by *SAYNOMORE*

Mob Ties 6

Lock Down Publications
P.O. Box 944
Stockbridge, Ga 30281
www.lockdownpublications.com

Copyright 2022 by SAYNOMORE
Mob Ties 6

All rights reserved. No part of this book may be reproduced in any form or by electronic or mechanical means, including information storage and retrieval systems without permission in writing from the publisher, except by a reviewer who may quote brief passages in review.
First Edition April 2022
Printed in the United States of America

This is a work of fiction. Names, characters, places, and incidents either are products of the author's imagination or are used fictitiously. Any similarity to actual events or locales or persons, living or dead, is entirely coincidental.

**Lock Down Publications
Like our page on Facebook: Lock Down Publications @
www.facebook.com/lockdownpublications.ldp**

Book interior design by: **Shawn Walker**
Edited by: **Nuel Uyi**

Saynomore

Stay Connected with Us!

Text **LOCKDOWN** to 22828 to stay up-to-date with new releases, sneak peaks, contests and more…

Thank you!

Submission Guideline.

Submit the first three chapters of your completed manuscript to ldpsubmissions@gmail.com, subject line: Your book's title. The manuscript must be in a .doc file and sent as an attachment. Document should be in Times New Roman, double spaced and in size 12 font. Also, provide your synopsis and full contact information. If sending multiple submissions, they must each be in a separate email.

Have a story but no way to send it electronically? You can still submit to LDP/Ca$h Presents. Send in the first three chapters, written or typed, of your completed manuscript to:

LDP: Submissions Dept
P.O. Box 944
Stockbridge, Ga 30281

DO NOT send original manuscript. Must be a duplicate.

Provide your synopsis and a cover letter containing your full contact information.

Thanks for considering LDP and Ca$h Presents.

Saynomore

Prologue

She looked out the window as the rain fell from the sky. She saw the flashing red and blue lights coming towards her establishment. She knew this day was coming for the last two weeks. All of her places of business had been raided. Detective Hall knew he couldn't trust anyone at his precinct. He'd gotten Cindy's witness statement and recording into the hands of the right people, and a domino effect started. Chief Tadem had Internal Affairs at the station going through all of the police records. Cindy Morris was in witness protection in an unknown location, and Symone had a warrant out for her arrest for the murder of Detective Deontay Boatman. Symone watched as the S.W.A.T team surrounded her business, and a spotlight shined directly on her as she looked out of her office window on the second floor, never flinching or losing her composure as she stared directly at them, then she heard the loud bullhorn.

"Symone Rose, we have a warrant for your arrest, for the murder of Detective Deontay Boatman. You have three minutes to come out with your hands up or we are coming in there to get you." Symone looked at the channel seven news helicopter fly above the police cars below as it recorded the event taking place live. She had both hands behind her back as she held her two Glock 9mm's.

***

Jamila was in her office watching everything on the news live. She couldn't believe what she was seeing. Her attention was drawn away from the TV to the door when Tasha walked in.

"Jamila, I was coming to tell you that Symone is on the news and that the police have her place surrounded now."

"I'm watching it now, Tasha, and I know that look in her eyes. She hasn't moved from the window yet, and her hand never left from behind her back. She doesn't plan on being taken alive. She plans on having a shoot-out."

"Jamila, do you really think she would do that? She has no win. She would be committing suicide."

Saynomore

"Tasha, I don't know what Symone is thinking, but she never surprises me." Jamila picked up the phone to call Symone.

***

Symone heard her phone going off, and walked backwards away from the window. She put one of her guns down on her desk so that she could answer her phone
"Hello."
"Symone, I know what you are thinking. Don't do it. You can beat this in court, trust me. But, if you go out in a shoot-out, you can hang your life up. You'll be looking at thirty years tops. Symone, please trust me. Lay your guns down and walk out the door. You'll be out in seventy-two hours tops. Symone, remember what I always taught you: intelligence over emotions."

Symone hung up the phone without saying anything, looking at the gun in her hand. She laid it down next to the gun already on her desk and walked out to her office and went downstairs. She opened the front door of Panache and looked at all of the police officers pointing their guns at her, as the local news helicopter had a spotlight on her.

The rain was pouring down, making puddles of water on the ground. Symone stepped through the doors outside as the police ran up to her and cuffed her on live TV. They walked her to the paddy wagon, put her inside and closed the door. Everyone watched as the paddy wagon drove off.

Chapter One

"District Attorney Kendrick, I see you have your fish on the hook."

"As we speak they are bringing her into custody right now, Mrs. West."

"Well, Kendrick, don't go popping bottles yet. You only have one witness who was under the influence of cocaine and alcohol but claims to have witnessed the murder of Detective Boatman at night in the dark with no street lights. Any decent attorney would eat this up at trial, and with the money that Symone Rose has and the pull that Jamila LaCross has, she's going to walk out that door within forty-eight hours, tops.

"You don't have to worry about that, Mrs. West, I have more than one trick up my sleeve."

"I hope you do, because I have a feeling that she's gonna walk out of the courtroom with two thumbs up like John Gotti."

Mrs. West patted District Attorney Kendrick two times on his shoulder before walking away. Kendrick looked at her before turning around and putting his key into his office door and opening it. Going into his office, he placed his briefcase on his desk and hung his coat up on the coat rack. He took a seat behind his desk and turned his computer on. He'd done his job and got the warrant for Symone, but he didn't just want her; he wanted Jamila too, and by the blood of his dead father he promised himself that he was going to get her too.

Saynomore

Chapter Two

Detective Hall sat in the back of the room as Special Agent Brooks spoke to the room with ten F.B.I agents and five D.E.A agents. "Listen up. Quiet. Pay attention. We have two sisters who've taken over New York City, leaving a body count behind them. They don't care who they kill. If you get in their way, you die. As of right now, Symone is operating in Brooklyn and Jamila is operating in Queens. Between the two of them their operations are supplying ninety percent of the drugs in New York City. They control two of the most dangerous mafia families that New York has ever witnessed. If you all will take a look to the right at the projector screen, the man that you see is Tony Lenacci. He was the head of most notorious mafia family in his era. There were attempts made on his life, both failed. He ran New York City from the 1970's to the early 2000's and was killed by this woman on the screen to the right, Jamila LaCross a.k.a Red Invee, in his own nightclub. Since then, the rise of Jamila—or should I say the LaCross family—began. There has been a countless body count that we can't prove, but we know that the LaCross family is responsible for it. As you see on the screen, there is a picture of everyone who has been killed since Jamila came on the scene. I'm going to read the names off from left to right for you: Mayor Oakland was killed at the Diamond Pad Hotel within seventy-two hours after delivering his speech, alongside two peace officers. Kent Washington was killed within a week's time after being elected into his seat in Congress. Detective Ross and Detective Ferguson were both killed protecting a witness of Mayor Oakland's assassination. We have Detective Green and Detective Boatman. Detective Boatman was shot twice in the head and chest and set on fire. It was a planned hit on his life. Detective Green was killed on a routine beat while he was checking out an abandoned warehouse, which we believe was another set-up, because Officer Roger was killed with the same gun as Detective Green forty-eight hours after Green's death—this came down from ballistics after Roger's autopsy. Officer Morris was killed at Southside hospital, shot in the head, and don't forget District Attorney Moore and his driver who was beheaded and chopped up and dropped off on the courthouse steps, the same as Officer Omar who was carved up like a pumpkin and dropped off. I'm not going to go over all of the officers who were killed or the details of how they were killed, but you all are familiar with all of the officers on the screen. As you look now you see some of the most notorious MOB figures that have been killed. I'm not going to go into the details about their deaths, but as you can see we have: Tony Lanacci, Chris Teliono, Alex Lanacci, Sonny Lanacci, and Sylvio Deniro. Listen, this list can go on and on and we'd waste valuable time naming all of these guys. There's a box right here. You guys see this box on this desk? I need four names in this box. I need two people to go undercover in the LaCross family and two people to go undercover in the Rose family. We need some solid evidence to nail their asses to the cross. That's the only way we're gonna get them. We know that both families have law enforcement officers working for them, so trust no one. I'm not going to say this is going to be easy. I'm not going to say this won't be a suicide mission because it is. I know some of you want to earn your stripes, but if this is what you really want to do, put your name in the box and come see me. For those of you who don't know, that's Detective Hall in the back and it is because of him that we are able to work this case and bring down Anthony Catwell's daughters. He knows how both families operate. He can give you the intel and background checks on them. Other than that, put your name in the box if you are interested in going undercover."

Chapter Three

"Kendrick, you can't be for real. Is this why you called me down to your office? You are basing your whole case on Symone Rose over a witness who was intoxicated the night of Detective Deontay Boatman's murder. You can't be serious, and to put more icing on the cake she has a criminal history for prostitution and possession of cocaine. There isn't a jury in New York City that will find my client guilty of murder with the strings you are trying to pull. The only thing you did was waste the taxpayers' money, so let me make this very clear, so that we will have an over-understanding, listen and watch me very closely."

District Attorney Kendrick watched as Symone Rose's attorney, Mr. Thompson, picked the sheet of paper up off the desk and ripped it in half in front of him.

"We respectfully decline your offer of twenty-five to life."

District Attorney Kendrick looked at Mr. Thompson as he mocked him in his office.

"Have it your way, Mr. Thompson, I'll see you at trial, and we'll let the people decide."

"We shall, so we shall, Kendrick. I'll see you in a little while at my client's bond hearing."

Kendrick watched as Mr. Thompson picked up a piece of candy off of his desk and walked out of his office door. District Attorney Kendrick rested his hands on his head. He knew without a doubt in his mind that Symone would walk out of that courtroom. He picked up the phone and called a friend for a favor.

"Hey, Raider, it's Kendrick, I'm calling for a favor."

***

Detective Hall looked at Symone through the double-sided window as she sat in the metal chair—not saying a word—when Special Agent Brooks walked into the room.

"Detective Hall, have you heard the news yet?"

"Yes, sir, a little while ago."

"We're going to get her, Hall, but we may have to let her go. She's all the way clean. Not even a parking ticket on her record."

"Sir, this woman is responsible for countless murders in New York City. She flooded the streets with drugs, and she had my friend gunned down in the streets in cold blood working on her case. Now I'm told she has a bond hearing coming up in the next few hours that we all know that she's going to make. I should've just killed her my fucking self, at least then I would have known that Green didn't die alone."

"Don't worry, Hall, we're going to get her, I can guarantee you that."

"Putting her behind bars is not justice for all the lives she took, mothers, fathers, brothers, sisters, sons, daughters all killed under her orders. She needs to die in the streets alongside her sister Jamila, preferably a public execution." Detective Hall looked at Special Agent Brooks one more time before walking out the door. He held the door for another agent to walk in.

"How is she looking, sir?"

"She hasn't moved from that one spot all day. She hasn't asked to speak to her lawyer. She's good, real good. She knows that her high priced attorney is already working on her case. I hate to say it but Detective Hall might have a point. The only real justice would be to be standing over her dead body in the streets, at least then we would know the monster in Brooklyn is dead, because no judge is going to convict her.

Chapter Four

Vinnie sat at his desk reading a newspaper and smoking a cigar.

"For years I've asked the question, who killed Detective Boatman? Not that I gave a fuck, because he was a piece of shit, but I should have known it was Rose. She made Jamaica, Queens the murder capital of the United States six years ago, Clark."

"So you think she's going to get the needle for this one, for killing Detective Boatman?"

"No, she's not even going to get convicted. She's already out on a one-hundred-thousand-dollar bond. My bet's she's already looking for this witness to have her ass smoked, and I'm also willing to bet that Red Invee has already paid the District Attorneys and the Judges to make this go away. This is gonna be a hung jury, or a dead-locked case. I can guarantee you that. You know what, Clark? Reach out to Rose and let her know that the Lenacci family is here to aid her in any way possible if need be."

"I'll get on that right away, boss."

Vinnie nodded and continued reading the paper about Detective Boatman's murder and the mafia family behind it.

***

"Symone, I'm trying to find out the whereabouts of this witness right now. The District Attorney is not trusting nobody with her location. Ever since Deniro's location was compromised and the killing of him on a prison transport bus, no officers will know the witnesses' location or where they're being held."

"Jamila, the only witness out there that night, I killed. I sat in the car and watched who was out there that night before I did anything, now six years later this bitch pops up out of nowhere."

Symone walked to the sliding glass doors in Jamila's office and opened them up. Jamila watched as Symone reached into her pocket and took out a *black and mild* and lit it. Symone stepped out onto the balcony as Jamila walked to the sliding doors and leaned against the door frame; she watched Symone look over the rail at the city of Queens.

"So now what? I just sit back and wait for this bitch to come and testify against me or what she claims she saw six years ago?"

"No, you go run Brooklyn. Don't nothing stop, but from now on you move more carefully, because you know you're under investigation from the local police department, the F.B.I., and the D.E.A. You just know that you are being watched. Don't worry about the witness. I have eyes looking for her now."

Symone flicked her *black and mild* over the rail. She turned around and looked at Jamila. She walked up to her and gave Jamila a hug and a kiss on the cheek. As she went to walk past, Jamila stopped her by placing her hand on her chest.

"Symone, don't worry about this domino effect, because one thing I know about a domino effect is—once the last domino falls, it's all over. Everyone that's a part of this investigation who is against you, you will be able to talk face to face, that I promise you." Jamila removed her hand from Symone's chest and nodded as Symone walked past her.

Chapter Five

"Chief Tadem, where is Detective Green's property? I can't find any of his files, police reports, or his records. His office is completely clean, wiped down as if it was a crime scene."

Chief Tadem pulled his cigar and looked at Officer August from Internal Affairs.

"Detective Hall packed up all of Detective Green's property. To my understanding he took all of the property to Internal Affairs office. That's why you're here now."

"Is that so, Chief Tadem?"

"Yes, it is, Officer August," Chief Tadem said as he leaned back in his chair, smoking his cigar.

"I think we are done here for today, Chief Tadem. I will see you tomorrow morning bright and early, to go over some more records and files."

Chief Tadem didn't say anything as he watched Officer August walk out of his office.

"The first chance I get, I swear, I'm going to kill that rat mutherfucker Hall." Chief Tadem put his cigar out and opened his desk drawer, picking up his car keys and putting on his jacket as he walked out of his office. He didn't say anything to anybody as he walked out of the police station. He put his duffel bag in the back seat of the car. He got in the front seat and lit his cigar. He looked at the precinct as he drove off. It was six p.m. when he made it to the crossway by his house. As he was about to drive off, he saw the headlights coming at him at full speed. He saw a flash and felt the impact as his car rolled over twice. He was dizzy as he looked up. He was still strapped into his car seat as his car was upside down. His vision was blurred as he unlatched his seat belt and fell to the ground. He looked up and saw a heavy-set man walking towards him, dressed in all black. Chief Tadem tried to crawl out of the broken car window. When he looked up, the last thing he saw was the boot coming down on his face knocking him out cold.

Saynomore

"It's time to pay the piper, Chief Tadem," Young Cap said with a crooked grin across his face, as he dragged Chief Tadem out of the car and put him in the back of the Hummer.

***

Detective Mayfield stepped under the yellow caution tape as he looked at Chief Tadem's car flipped upside down. He walked up to the trail of broken glass where he could tell that Chief Tadem's body had been dragged. He walked over to the broken window, kneeled down and looked at the drops of blood on the broken glass. He looked in the back of the car and noticed that Chief Tadem's duffel bag had not been removed. He stood up and walked over to the reporting officer on the scene.

"Officer Gates, you were the first officer to arrive on the scene, correct?"

"Yes, I was, sir."

"Where were you when dispatch called it in over the radio about the crash?"

"I was about fifteen minutes away, just coming up on Riverside Drive. By the time I got here, Chief Tadem was gone and everything was the way that you see it now."

"I can tell, officer, whoever hit Chief Tadem's car knew what they were doing. You know what I also noticed—that there is some red paint on the front fender of the car, so that tells me we are looking for a red truck or van. If you noticed, Chief Tadem's duffel bag is at the back of the car on the ground. Whoever hit his car didn't take it. Whoever did this has been watching him. This was a kidnapping, a snatch and grab, the way I see it. We have twenty-four hours to find him before they kill him, and then we'll be called to identify the body."

"Who do you think did this, detective?"

"I don't know, but the question I'm asking myself is *'why did they do it*?', and what are they preventing him from talking about, or was he a loose string to an even bigger case?" Detective Mayfield walked back to Chief Tadem's car after talking to the officer, to look over the scene again.

Saynomore

Chapter Six

Cindy sat on the couch with her knees to her chest and her arms wrapped around them as she watched the news.
"She's coming for me; I know she is."
"Ms. Morris, she doesn't even know where you are at."
"She will find me. Look what just happened to Chief Tadem, someone took him, and he's a cop. I knew this was gonna happen."
"Ms. Morris, we don't even know if that's the case."
"I'm not stupid, detective, she's out there somewhere with a bullet with my name on it."
"I'm not gonna let her hurt you at all, I promise you that. I will protect you."
"You can't protect me, no one can, she just had a cop kidnapped. She's coming and we both know it."
"Let her come. I have a bullet with her name on it, when she does come."
Cindy got up off the couch, picked up the remote control and turned the TV off.
"I'll bet Chief Tadem said the same thing, now look at him, hoping someone will come save him," Cindy said as she walked off to her room.

***

Gino Sabrano walked into the casino with three of his men. They stopped at the door as Gino Sabrano looked around.
"Come on, let's go see Ms. Rose," Gino said, as he saw Iceman coming down the stairs to meet them.
"Mr. Sabrano, how are you today?"
"Fairly well, Iceman."
"That's good to hear."
"Is Ms. Rose around?"
"Yes, she's in her office. Follow me and I will take you to see her."

Saynomore

Gino Sabrano opened his palm in a friendly gesture, letting Iceman know 'after you'. Iceman opened Symone's office door. She was standing with her back towards them as she looked out her office window. She turned around and looked at Gino Sabrano as he walked into her office, then she started walking towards him.

"Mr. Sabrano, this is a surprise. I had no idea you were coming by. How are you?"

"I'm fine, Ms. Rose, but the question is *how are you*?"

"I'm good, stressed, but I'm fine."

"Well, don't be stressed. I don't need you to be worried. You will never be convicted of these charges. I can guarantee you that."

"That's good to hear, because my first court arraignment is next week."

"Symone, you are a made woman, remember that. You know, I never had an encounter with this Detective Deontay Boatman, but I have heard stories about him and from what I've been told, he was quite a character."

Symone just looked as Mr. Sabrano talked, while they stood in the middle of her office floor.

"I remember seeing the news a few years back and how he was killed in the worst way, how they had no suspects to his murder. Now the story comes out how mafia boss Symone Rose is responsible for Detective Boatman's murder. Ms. Rose, you never seem to surprise me. Here, I have something for you, take this card, Mr. Alexander Foster will represent you at trial. This attorney costs $30,000 an hour." Symone took the black card with the gold writing on it and looked at it.

"Don't worry, he's already overpaid, Rose."

"Mr. Sabrano, thank you so much for all that you are doing for me."

"Rose, you are my personally-made woman, and that's all that needs to be said. Now Rose, I have to be going. I just wanted to hand you that card personally."

"Thank you again, Mr. Sabrano." Symone watched as Iceman walked Mr. Sabrano out of her office and back to his limo. She walked to her desk and picked up her office phone and dialed the number that was on the card.

Saynomore

Chapter Seven

Mrs. West stormed into District Attorney Kendrick's office and slammed the newspaper on his desk as he was on the phone. She stood over him and looked at him.

"Let me call you back. I have to take care of something."

"I saw the news about Chief Tadem's disappearance," Mrs. West said as soon as District Attorney Kendrick ended the call.

"What does that have to do with me, Katrina?" District Attorney Kendrick retorted.

"Everything. You wanted Symone Rose and her sister Jamila LaCross so bad you had a warrant taken out on her over a non-reliable witness that claims she saw a detective get killed six years ago, who was a crooked detective we all know was a piece of shit."

"Come on, Katrina, don't come in here, my office, trying to insinuate that Chief Tadem's kidnapping or disappearance—whatever you want to call it—is somehow connected to my case against Symone Rose."

"Kendrick, if you don't open your damn eyes and see that this is bigger than Symone Rose—Kendrick, this is called the hush game. We don't trust you in court so we're going to shoot you up ourselves. Connect the damn dots, Kendrick, connect the dots. Detective Hall goes to Internal Affairs against Chief Tadem, Chief Tadem and his police department goes under investigation, your witness goes into protective custody, you get a warrant taken out for the arrest of Symone Rose over Detective Deontay Boatman's murder, the same Chief of Police, Tadem who didn't go forward with this witnesses' statement when it was presented to him gets into an accident where his vehicle is flipped over. All of a sudden he is missing when shit hits the fan. Connect the dots, Kendrick, it's the hush game."

"That's some bullshit, Katrina, and you know it. There's no such thing as the hush game."

"You're so blind with the hatred that you have for Symone Rose and Jamila LaCross, it's overpowering the love you have for your wife and kids, your family. If you know like I know, you had better keep an eye on your wife and kids, and if you don't know by now, your little star witness is already dead, she just don't know it yet. When you decided to put a crackhead up against Symone Rose, the dice aren't going to roll your way." Frowning, Mrs. West walked out of Kendrick's office. Kendrick picked up the newspaper that was on his desk and looked to where Katrina had circled the article about Chief Tadem and his picture in red.

***

Chief Tadem sat in a metal chair with his hands chained behind his back. His head was leaning forward. He heard the sound of someone walking on twigs and leaves. The room was pitch-black. He couldn't see two feet in front of his own face. His back and side was hurting from the car crash; he felt bugs crawling all over him.

He knew nobody was going to find him. He knew he was a dead man. The doors opened up and the light blinded him, that's when he heard the last voice he would ever hear.

"I hope you made your peace with God these last few hours."

Young Cap walked up to Chief Tadem and pointed the Mossberg shotgun at his head.

"I've already made my peace with God."

"Good then." Young Cap didn't say anything else. He pulled the trigger, splattering Chief Tadem's brains on the metal wall. Young Cap looked at Chief Tadem's half head that was left on his body as he walked out of District Attorney Kendrick's rental property shed, leaving Chief Tadem's dead body there with the shed doors open.

Chapter Eight

District Attorney Kendrick walked to the back of the restaurant and sat at the end table across from Raider, a private investigator, whom he'd asked a favor from. It was 7 a.m.

"Thank you for doing this for me, Raider."

"No problem, Kendrick."

"So, what do you have for me? I have to be in court in an hour."

"Honestly, nothing. I've been following Symone Rose for the past two weeks. The only person that she's with constantly is her driver. He picks her up at seven o'clock in the morning, takes her to all of her establishments, and he drops her off back home no later than nine p.m."

"You mean to tell me that you didn't see her conversing with anybody?"

"I followed her into the casino and the strip club. When she goes into the casino, she walks in and goes behind private doors that leads to her private office, and it's the same thing with the strip club. Besides her driver, there's no one else."

"You got to be fucking kidding me."

"Kendrick, she knows she's being watched, she's not stupid. Now, I will tell you this, something *did* make me raise an eyebrow two days ago."

"And what was that?"

"Guess who went to the casino hours after Symone Rose was dropped off there."

"I don't know, tell me."

"Gino Sabrano."

"You're telling me Gino Sabrano, the head Don, Gino Sabrano."

"That is exactly what I am telling you." Raider passed him pictures of Gino Sabrano and three of his men walking into the casino.

"Raider, do you think that this is somehow related to Symone Rose? Why he went there?"

"Kendrick, Gino Sabrano has been off the scene for over two decades, and now he's back, and more importantly going into one

Saynomore

of Symone Rose's establishments. You ask yourself, what are the odds?"

"Raider, do you have any pictures of them together?"

"No, but I do have some pictures of Iceman walking him through those private doors I was telling you about earlier. Here they are right here, and here are some more pictures of Iceman walking them back out of the casino a half hour later. She's smart, Kendrick, she's not going to let herself be seen with anybody, but this is what I will tell you, if Gino Sabrano is involved somehow, you need to watch out for yourself. He's very powerful and very dangerous. Now, I've rode this train as far as I'm going to take it, I hope I was a help to you."

"Thanks, Raider, you were a help to me."

Raider patted Kendrick on the back two times before walking out of the restaurant, leaving Kendrick looking at the pictures he took for him.

***

It was nine a.m. when Symone's limo pulled up to the front of the courthouse. There were two local news teams outside of the courthouse airing live. There was a photographer taking pictures for the local newspapers. The outside of the courthouse was a madhouse with all of the commotion going on, and the excitement over the Symone Rose trial. Symone stepped out of the limo looking like a model. All eyes were on her. She had on a white three-piece suit, with two-inch stiletto heels. Her hair was pulled to the back in a bun, with a pair of dark shades covering her face as she walked up to her attorney—Alexander Foster.

"How are you feeling, Ms. Rose."

"Better, I just want to get this day over with."

"I understand, let me prepare you now. The District Attorney Kendrick is going to paint a picture about you to the judge. He's gonna make you look like a monster, but don't worry about that. Do you know how cases are won in court?"

"No, tell me, Mr. Foster."

"It's all about who can tell a better story. I just need you to sit quietly and look innocent for me. Don't worry about the people in there or the cameras, you got me?"

"Yeah, I got you."

"Now, turn around and wave at the people. They're here for you." Symone sat in the courtroom and listened to District Attorney Kendrick go on and on about the crime rate in Brooklyn, drug trafficking and countless murders.

"Your honor, sitting here in the courtroom is Symone Rose. She is the head of the most notorious mafia family in Brooklyn. The Rose family. As she sits there looking innocent, I am here today to show you why Symone Rose's bond should be revoked, and she should be remanded into custody immediately. She is a flight risk, and I have a witness who can place her at the scene of the crime where Detective Deontay Boatman was killed. Not only that, but said that she (Symone Rose) was the trigger woman behind his brutal murder six years ago. Symone Rose has no value for human life, and she does not respect the laws of our city."

"OK. District Attorney Kendrick, you may take your seat now. Your argument, Attorney Foster."

Alexander Foster looked at Symone and winked as he stood up.

"Your honor, my client, Symone Rose, has been an upstanding citizen for the twenty-eight years that she has been walking this earth. She doesn't even have a jay-walking ticket on her record. Nothing that District Attorney Kendrick said here today was an actual true statement. Where is the proof behind his allegations? This alleged witness, which is District Attorney Kendrick's trump card, who admits she was on cocaine, and under the influence of alcohol, on the said night that Detective Deontay Boatman was killed. Not only that, your honor, she has a criminal history of possession of cocaine and prostitution. District Attorney Kendrick's whole case is based on the testimony of this alleged witness who claims she saw Detective Boatman's murder six years ago. There is no proof that my client is the head of any mafia family. District Attorney

Kendrick has no proof of what he is saying is true. Besides this unreliable witness, is there anything else that can be proven to be a fact against Symone Rose, my client?"

"You may take your seat, Mr. Foster."

"District Attorney Kendrick, do you have any proof of the allegations that you have made against Symone Rose here today in my courtroom, other than your witness?"

"Not at this time, your honor."

"OK. Symone Rose will remain free on bond, until there is a set date for trial. Until then this court is adjourned."

Symone stood up and looked at her attorney and shook his hand, then she looked at District Attorney Kendrick and smiled at him. As she walked out of the courthouse, she waved at the people and threw two thumbs up and smiled.

Chapter Nine

Jamila watched as Symone walked out of the courthouse on the news. She started smiling when she saw Symone throw two thumbs up; that's when Tasha walked into her office.

"I see things worked out today for Symone in court."

"Yeah, thumbs up."

"Well, here you go, Jamila, this came for you in the mail today." Jamila looked at the brown box that Tasha handed her.

"Thank you. Did you check up on the new shipment this week?"

"Yes, I did. Masi has everything sealed and accounted for and ready to be shipped out."

"That's good. I'm glad to hear that, that's right on time." Jamila took a time out to look into the box and saw Chief Tadem's badge. She closed the box back and slid it to the side.

"Tasha, just have Masi hold everything in place. It's too hot right now to try and move anything with everything that's going on with the Detective Boatman murder trial. We don't have any room for slip-ups. I want eyes everywhere. If you see a car that's been parked on the street too long, have somebody go check it out. I want everyone that comes to my place of business watched at all times. I've been in this position before. The feds will send the Pope to your door if they know you will let him in. Remember this, Tasha, we're not on trial, but if they can link Red Invee to Rose, they'll nail their mothers to the cross for that celebration. So, I need you to be my eyes and ears at all times."

"I'm about to go take care of everything you asked me to do, Red Invee."

"Tasha, thank you."

"No problem."

Jamila watched as Tasha walked out of her office, she then picked up the phone and made a call.

***

Agent Brooks sat at his desk going over two files, when there was a knock at his office door.

"Come in." He looked and saw two agents walk into his office.

"So you think you two are ready to try to infiltrate the LaCross or the Rose family?"

"Sir, with the utmost respect, I've been in the streets my whole life. I'm from Philly. I can adapt to anything. I know I can infiltrate one of the families with no problems."

"You sound real confident, Corey, but this ain't no street gang. This is the mob. They'll kill your family and make you watch. They will peel your skin back to get the information they want to know. This is not a picnic. This is walking into hell's kitchen, so give me an apron and your order and I'll have your plate ready for you in an hour." Agent Brooks nodded at Corey.

"What about you, Melissa?"

"I know what I can do, sir, if you give me a chance, let my actions speak for themselves."

"You know, I'm going to go against my better judgement because I like the confidence that you two have. OK. Since you two want the assignments, I'm gonna see what you two can do. I'm assigning you to the Rose family, Melissa—and you've got the LaCross family, Corey. Go see Agent Malone, he'll set you both up with new identifications and backgrounds. Let him know I sent you."

"Thank you, sir, for this opportunity, we won't let you down," Corey and Melissa said in unison.

"I hope not, because your life is on the line. Literally."

Agent Brooks picked up the files, opened his desk drawer and dropped them inside as they walked out of his office.

Chapter Ten

Alexander Foster was on his phone in his office when Attorney Thompson walked into his office. Alexander held up one finger, gesturing for Attorney Thompson to hold on for a second, as he finished up his phone call. Brian Thompson took a seat in front of his desk, picked up the newspaper that was lying there and started reading it.

"My apologies, Mr. Thompson," Alexander said as he reached across his desk to shake Mr. Thompson's hand.

"How are you, Brian?"

"I'm well, and yourself?"

"I'm making it, that's all that matters."

"So, Mr. Foster, you asked me to come to your office. What can I do for you? Since you took over my case."

Alexander took his glasses off and put them down in front of him on his desk, and leaned forward as he looked at Mr. Thompson.

"I called you down here to put you back on the case. I want to make a dream team and I want you to play on it with me."

"Why is that? You don't need a dream team. This is an open and closed case."

"You're right, but that's not the big picture I want you to see. I want to crush District Attorney Kendrick to the point where he can never make a comeback. Think of the publicity we will get out of this case. This is a high profile case. This is the O.J. Simpson trial all over again, and I'll give you a 40/60 split. You'll be back on the chase and in the limelight with me. So, what do you say?"

"I say, I'm glad to be on the team, so, what's the angle we're looking at?"

Alexander looked at Brian and smiled.

"Corruption."

"I like that."

***

Saynomore

District Attorney Kendrick pulled up to his rental house. He had a good friend who came down from Rochester, New York to help him on the case. He was going to let his friend and his family stay at his rental house while he was in Brooklyn helping on the Rose case. When he pulled up, he saw Kevin leaning up against his car right outside of the house.

"Kevin, thank you for coming. I really need you on this one."

"That's what friends are for. I've been keeping updates on the case and the events surrounding it."

"Kevin, this case is my nightmare. Everything about it is wrong."

"Well, look, I'm down here now. Show me around the house, and let me get my things moved in and we can tackle everything tomorrow morning head on."

"Sure, come on, that sounds like a plan to me."

"It's a four-bedroom house, two baths, a full basement. Let me show you how the basement looks. There are no rooms here, just an open space, a place to plug in your washer and dryer, it's very cool down here in the summer."

"Yeah, I like it down here. It's a place where my girls can come and play."

"Well, come on, let me show you the shed in the backyard, it's where I keep all the lawn equipment."

"Kendrick, this is a nice sized backyard."

"Yeah, that's another reason I bought this property. The trees and the hedges block out the neighbors so they can see into my yard."

"Kendrick, do you always keep your shed open?"

"No, I haven't been here in weeks. There was a lock on there."

District Attorney Kendrick stopped and looked around his back yard as Kevin walked toward the open shed.

"Holy shit!" Kevin said as he ran from the shed and dropped to his knees, throwing up in front of Kendrick.

"What the hell did you just see?"

Kevin pointed to the shed, not saying a word. When Kendrick walked to the shed, he looked and saw Chief Tadem's dead body

being eaten by raccoons. He covered his mouth and ran from the shed, pulling out his cell phone. Kevin looked up at Kendrick.
"What the fuck did you get yourself into, Kendrick?"

45 Minutes Later—

Kendrick watched as CSI officers walked around his house dusting for fingerprints, taking pictures of everything.
"Kendrick, this was a message to you. I overheard them say that his body has been sitting in there for over a week. Look, I'm still going to help you on this case, but I can't move my family into this house. I'm going to find a place to stay and I'll be in touch sometime this week, buddy," Kevin said as he walked off.
Kendrick knew what Kevin had said was right, but he was in too deep with this case to walk away now.

Saynomore

Chapter Eleven

Pistol watched as a young female sat in the back of the strip club, taking shot after shot of Cîroc like she always did. He'd never had a conversation with her. He just watched her for the past two weeks when she came in on Fridays and Saturdays.

"Yo, Kilo, come here for a second."

"What's up, Pistol?"

"What do you think about babygirl in the corner over there?"

"I don't know what to make of her."

"She been coming in here the last few weeks, sitting in the same corner, posted up by herself."

"You think shit funny with her, like something's up with her?"

"I don't know. I'm about to pull up on her now, watch the floor."

"For sure, I got you."

Pistol walked over where she was sitting at taking shots of Cîroc.

"Can I sit with you, baby girl?"

"That's up to you."

"So where are you from?"

"Long Island, why do you ask?"

"Because I never saw you before, until a few nights ago."

"So what? You got twenty-one questions for me or something? Let me find out you watching me."

"I can say the same thing about you. What's your name?"

"Kia, and yours?"

"Pistol. Come on, Kia, let's go up to the VIP."

"Kia watched as Pistol got up. She got up and followed him to the VIP area. Kilo watched as they walked up the stairs.

"I see y'all poppin big boy bottles up here."

"Welcome to the big boy table, little momma," Kilo said.

Kia laughed.

"Hold up," Kia said and reached into her pocket and pulled out a stack of hundreds.

"I get a check too, big boy."

"We got us a paper chaser, Pistol," Kilo said, nodding at her.

"I see, facts, baby girl got some business about herself."

Pistol heard the back door open. When he turned around, he saw Perk G walking in the door with a book bag over his shoulders.

"Peace, Pistol."

"Peace, Perk, I didn't expect you tonight," Pistol said.

"That's the way Rose want it from now on, just pop up, drop off, and pick up. She said you had that ready for me since last night."

"Yeah, I do."

"Let me get that so I can push on."

"Hold on, Perk—Kilo, take Kia downstairs while I take care of this business."

Kia looked at Perk, got up and walked through the doors, headed downstairs with Kilo.

"Yo, who is she?"

"Nobody, right now. So what Rose got for me?"

"Ten kilos right now. When you get this off, just hit my line and I'll be through to pick the money up within seventy-two hours. What you got for me?"

"Two hundred grand." Pistol walked to the cabinet and pulled out the duffle bag and handed it to Perk.

"I'm out. I got to go see Iceman now. Stay up, Pistol."

"Copy that, bruh." Pistol watched as Perk G walked back out the door. Pistol looked at Kia as she was handing one of the strippers money on stage. He took a shot of Cîroc and waved them both back up to the VIP.

***

Mrs. West walked into Kendrick's office. She knocked so hard on the door before she opened it, it made him jump.

"Don't go shitting bricks now, Kendrick, you wanted this case. Now you have it."

"It is too late in the day for you to be coming in here with that 'I fucking told you so', Katrina. I have a lot of shit on my plate, not to mention I had a dead fucking cop in my shed being eaten by raccoons."

"Shit, better your shed than mine, and this isn't even the tip of the iceberg yet. Well, you wanted the boogey man or woman. Well, he or she just stepped out of the closet, and I can promise you this, this isn't the case you wanted." Katrina looked at the door as Kevin walked into the office.

"My apologies, did I interrupt anything?"

"No, you didn't, Kevin, this is D.A. Katrina West. Katrina, this is Kevin. He's here to help me out on the case."

"Nice to meet you, Katrina." Kevin extended his hand to shake hers.

"Likewise, Kevin. I see Kendrick dragged you into this nightmare, but I hope you enjoy the party," Katrina said as she walked out of the office, closing the door behind her.

"She is different," Kevin said.

"Kevin, she can really be our handful, but don't worry about Katrina. You'll get to know her over time. So, what's that you have in your hands, Kevin?"

"Symone Rose's files. I want to read up on her to know who I'm dealing with. This can't be the female you've told me about, because what I've read doesn't match up to what you've told me."

"Yeah, she's clean all the way on paper, but I promise you, she's a cold-hearted killer." Kendrick opened his desk drawer and handed him Jamila's file.

"Read her file. That's her sister—Jamila LaCross a.k.a. Red Invee, and tell me what you think."

Chapter Twelve

Iceman sat at his desk looking at the ten kilos of heroin that Perk G brought him last night. He knew the feds was watching them, but that wasn't gonna stop him from getting his money. That's when Halo came walking through the door.

"I see that Perk G was able to make the drop off to you last night."

"Yeah, he did."

"How long do you think it'll take you to get off of all of it?"

"About two weeks at the most."

"Good, because we are trying to get everything off. We get it, we push it off and then on to the next load. We can't afford to keep nothing until the prices go down. There is too much heat on our family right now."

"I know. Rose has become a ghost. I don't even see her like I used to."

"It's for the best right now. Shit really got bananas when Red Invee had Chief Tadem bodied inside D.A. Kendrick's shed. Red Invee delivered the message to the D.A. who is working Rose's case, but at the same time dropped the bomb on us."

"Halo, this the life we signed up for. This shit gonna blow over."

"Yeah, you're right, but how long before it does, Iceman? Now that's the question. But look, I'm out, I have some more runs to make. I'll see you in two weeks, homie."

"Yo, stay up, Halo, and I got you as soon as I get this shit off." Iceman picked up the kilos and placed them in a duffel bag inside the closet before walking off.

Saynomore

Chapter Thirteen

Gino Sabrano sat in his living room reading the newspaper. The headline read: "Could This Be New York City's Deadliest Trial?" To the right of the newspaper was a picture of Symone Rose from her first court appearance. He stopped reading the paper when two of his bodyguards walked Vinnie Lenacci into his living room. Gino folded his newspaper and sat it down on his coffee table.

"Vinnie, come have a seat and tell me what was so important that you needed to come talk to me about today, that I had to reschedule my fly fishing appointment until next week."

"Mr. Sabrano, both of our families have had its time at the top of the pyramid."

"We did, so what's your point?"

"Since Red Invee came to the table, there have been more F.B.I cases against the families than ever before, F.B.I and D.E.A agents being killed, D.A.'s being beheaded, detectives being shot and set on fire, the Chief of police being murdered inside a District Attorney's shed. We all know that Tony was for himself, but there were no wars in the streets, and law enforcement men and women weren't being killed. There are rules, and Red Invee and Rose just think they are above them. If we don't do something soon, we are all going to fall with secret indictments that will bring all of us down, and I don't want to be on that boat when it sinks. Plus, when do Italians, us, start taking orders from Negros?"

"Vinnie, you make a lot of good points, but with different times comes different changes. You shouldn't worry about F.B.I cases or secret indictments. Rose is gonna beat all charges, and Red Invee delivered a strong message to the D.A. 's office. What Red Invee and Rose are doing is putting the fear back in New York City from the mob, something Tony forgot to do. That's why you had this detective Boatman running around extorting families, making the mafia pay dues. Now look at him, dead because of Rose."

Everyone who sat at the head of the table after me failed the families, except for Red Invee. She bought more political protection to the families, she made a better economy for the mob, and she put the fear that was needed back in New York City, who forgot who we are. Let me stamp this so you know where we stand: Red Invee and Rose are *made* females, not one hair on their heads better not come up missing. The Lenacci family had their time on top of the pyramid, now it's over, so sit in the back seat and enjoy the ride. Now, if you don't mind, since I cancelled my fly fishing appointment, I'd like to finish reading my paper. Gentlemen, will you please escort Mr. Lenacci to his car?"

Vinnie didn't say anything. He got up and walked out of the house to his car. Gino picked up his paper and started reading it, knowing that Vinnie was going to be a problem.

***

Kevin sat at his desk, reading over Jamila LaCross' file when D.A. Kendrick walked in.

"Kendrick, what is more important to you? Your family or your career?"

"Why would you ask me that? My family, of course."

"Then you need to walk away from this case. Don't try to be the D.A. to bring down Jamila LaCross and Symone Rose. I'm telling you as a friend, walk away."

"So, I guess you plan on backing out of this case on me?"

"No, I'm not, but if anything comes to my family or my little girls, then I will walk away, before I let them get hurt or traumatized."

"I respect that, Kevin."

"Kendrick, this is just like you. Growing up, you had to fight the biggest guy in the streets, now you have to go after the most dangerous mafia families to try and prove a point."

"It's not that, Kevin, all I want is justice for the families that lost loved ones."

"Kendrick, you can wipe your ass and tell me that it's not shit, and what you just said is some bullshit. You want to be the D.A. that brought Anthony Catwell's daughters down. Come on, let's get to it, we got a lot of work to get done if we want anything to stick to them in the courtroom."

Saynomore

Chapter Fourteen

Vinnie pulled out a picture of his daughter from her fifteenth birthday party. It killed him inside to know she cried for his help and there was nothing he could do to save her life as he watched her get beheaded right in front of his eyes while Red Invee commanded it. There was no doubt in his mind that Red Invee was gonna die and he was going to be the one to kill her. He placed his daughter's picture back in his pocket when he heard a knock at his office door.

"Come in."

"Hey, Vinnie, I was coming to see how the meeting went with Gino."

"He's siding with the Negros. He made that clear as water to me. So to kill her, we first have to kill him. Deniro had the right plan, he just went about it wrong."

"So, how do you want it done, boss?"

"We need to make it look like an accident. With everything going on with Rose's trial, the fucking Chief of police who got killed—it shouldn't be no problem setting this up the way it needs to be, and if we can't make this look like an accident then it'll just be a bloody homicide." Vinnie leaned back in his chair and lit his cigar.

"Molly, I don't need this getting out. Get one person you can trust and get the job done." Molly nodded and walked out of the office.

***

Jamila looked out of her back window as she talked to Tasha.

"Tasha, you know what I used to stress to Lorenzo?"

"No, tell me."

The city of Queens, Tasha, I used to stress to Lorenzo the city of Queens. The LaCross family is loved by few, hated by many and respected by all. This is a new day and a new time. Loyalty is just a word to people now, honor doesn't even exist anymore, and trust will get you killed. Tasha, we have a deadline. What I want you to do is go see Young Cap and let him know to be ready for the second grocery list to be eaten when I give him the address."

"I'll go do that now, Mrs. LaCross." As Tasha turned around to walk out the door, Masi walked in the door with Muscle.

"You two come in and have a seat. I need a job done and I want it done right. I know a cop when I see one. I been doing this too long not to know. Walk with me to the VIP now, look at the second table to the right. You see that gentleman, this is the third time he has eaten here, plus he has been to *Destiny's*. From what I've been told, he's been trying to shop with us as well. Come back to my office now. They put a new jack in the field up against me, and if they put one up against me then I know they did the same thing to Rose."

"So, what do you want us to do to him?"

"Invite him into the family, show him around, show him a good time. Don't talk about any family business around him, bring him to *Passions*, but don't take him to the waste plant. Set him up with a room at *Destiny's* if he needs a place to stay. Your job is to find out what he knows; after that, we do what we do with rats—we exterminate them. All we're doing is setting up a rat trap, so you two go take care of that now. I have a phone call I have to make."

Chapter Fifteen

Detective Mayfield walked into Agent Brooks' office to see him talking to Detective Hall.

"Detective Mayfield, please come in and have a seat and join us. So let me catch you up on things. We are not making a big deal about Chief Tadem's murder out loud. We have two agents working both families undercover, and from what I was told, one of our agents already made contact with one of the families."

"With the utmost respect, Mr. Brooks," Detective Mayfield began, "you sent two agents into hell's kitchen and if you don't pull them out, you will be paying their loved ones a visit with a folded up flag. I have studied Red Invee, and what I know about her is that she's very smart, Chief Tadem's murder was a message to the witness and the D.A., you have two sisters running two of the most feared mafia families in New York City."

"So, Detective Hall, how do you think we should go about getting them?" asked Detective Mayfield.

"I don't know, but what I do know is that it's only a matter of time before she figures out who your agents are, then we'll be getting called to identify his or her body," said Agent Hall. Agent Brooks turned his attention to Detective Hall.

"What is your input, Detective Hall?" Agent Brooks asked him.

"If Jamila was in the lion's den when Daniel went in there, he would have been eaten. Symone is more ruthless than Jamila. If we're going to catch one of them slipping, it would be Rose. She's more careless than Red Invee. She would be our way through the door."

"Look, it's three of us here, let's put our cards on the table. We are taking a gamble to get these bitches off the streets," said Agent Brooks.

***

Symone's limo pulled up in front of the court house. There were people holding up signs that read: 'Symone Rose is innocent of all charges'. Other signs read: 'Symone is Brooklyn's Angel'. The New York City police department was out in front of the courthouse making sure no one crossed the barriers. When Symone stepped out of her limo, everyone started clapping and cheering for her. She waved to the crowd as she walked into the court house. All eyes were on her when she walked into the courtroom. She looked around at everyone as she took her seat next to her attorney. Her attorney, Alexander Foster, leaned over and whispered in her ear.

"The D.A.'s office sent me everything they have on you, and the strongest argument they have is the one witness, everything else is hearsay. They can't even get you on tax evasion. So, this is how we are going to fight this case. I'm going to argue how discreditable the witness is and Attorney Thompson is going to argue everything else. The odds are in our favor right now. Get ready to stand up, the judge is about to come in."

The bailiff walked into the courtroom and announced:

"All rise for Judge Mills Walker!" Everyone stood up.

"You may be seated. District Attorney Kendrick, you may begin with your opening statement," said Judge Mills Walker. District Attorney Kendrick walked over to a white board he had covered with a sheet, and uncovered it.

"Ladies and gentlemen, would you please turn your attention to this picture. The picture you see here is of Detective Deontay Boatman. He was murdered six years ago, shot six times and then he was set on fire. What I'm about to show the court may be a little graphic, but you must understand Symone Rose doesn't have any value for human life." District Attorney Kendrick removed the first picture of Detective Boatman, and behind that picture was a picture of his burned body after the fire department put the fire out.

The jurors and people in the courtroom covered their eyes and their mouths in shock at what they saw. District Attorney Kendrick put the first picture of Detective Boatman back on the board, covering the second picture.

"Ladies and Gentlemen of the jury, I know that picture was disturbing, but the female who is responsible for Detective Boatman's murder, that is who is on trial today. Symone Rose. That is all I have, your honor. Thank you."

"Attorney Alexander Foster, you may proceed with your opening statement," said Judge Walker.

"Thank you, your honor. Ladies and Gentlemen of the jury, we are all deeply sorry for what happened to Detective Deontay Boatman, but today we have the wrong person on trial here. My client, Symone Rose, is on trial over a witness' statement that is six years old. Not to mention, the witness honestly and openly admitted in her statement that she was intoxicated from the use of cocaine. She also stated that she was under the influence of alcohol, and this happened at night on a street with no street lights, and also the witness stated that she was one hundred yards away from the victim at the time of his murder. Ladies and Gentlemen of the jury, there are four serious points that we have to look at here. One, the witness was under the influence of alcohol; two, the witness was intoxicated from using an illegal street drug which was cocaine; three, the witness stated she was one hundred feet away from the scene and four, there were no streetlights on the street the crime took place on. So, how could the witness honestly identify my client as the person who committed this murder. That is what I need you, the jury, to take into consideration." Alexander Foster looked at Symone, then he looked at the judge.

"That will be all, your honor."

"OK, Mr. Foster, you may take your seat."

After an hour and a half, the judge called a recess until the following day. Symone stood up and looked at Cindy, and winked her eye at her as she walked out of the courtroom.

Saynomore

Chapter Sixteen

Detective Hall pulled into his driveway and opened the trunk of his car and pulled out his duffel bag. He looked around before opening the front door to his house. He unlocked his front door and stepped inside. That's when he felt a hard blow to the head and dropped to one knee. He looked up and was struck again. The strike dropped him to the floor. When he looked up, he saw a man dressed in all black looking at him.

"Who the fuck are you?" Detective Hall asked.

"The Grim Reaper, motherfucker," the other replied, "and I'm here for you fucking soul." Young Cap moved to kick Detective Hall in the face, but Detective Hall grabbed his foot and swung it, knocking it off balance, then he got up off the floor and charged him, knocking him over the living room table.

"Well, 'Grim Reaper', I'm sending you back to hell today. You fucked with the wrong nigga."

"Motherfucker, I am hell." Young Cap pulled out his .45 caliber and started shooting at Detective Hall. Detective Hall took two rounds to the chest, the shots knocking him down, but he managed to get up and skedaddled away. Young Cap tried to get up off the floor but slipped and fell back down. By the time he got up off of the floor, and went to look for Detective Hall, he was gone. By the time he made it to the front door, all he saw was the tail lights of Detective Hall's car as he was driving off. Young Cap ran into the middle of the street and started shooting at Detective Hall's car until he could no longer see it. He looked around and walked back into Detective Hall's house, picked up the duffel bag and left.

***

"Detective Hall, what the hell happened out there?" Detective Mayfield asked him.

"I pulled up to my house. I opened my front door and I was attacked. I was hit upside my head. I fell down, I fought him off me, I flipped him through my living room table, but he was fast on the draw. He let off two rounds to my chest. I'm lucky I had my vest on. My pistol slid under the loveseat when we were fighting. I grabbed my keys off the floor, got in my car and got out of there. I looked in my rearview mirror as he started shooting at me."

"Detective Hall, what did he look like? Can you describe him for me?"

"I couldn't tell you. It was dark, but I can tell you he was heavyset and above six feet tall. He weighed about three hundred pounds."

"OK. I have C.S.I at your house right now looking for fingerprints and anything else that will help us catch this guy. I hate to say it, but you've been targeted, someone wants you dead."

"Sir, let's not fool ourselves, it's either Rose or Red Invee that sent a hit out on me. He called himself the 'Grim Reaper'."

"Look, Detective, relax right now, and tomorrow I want a full report on everything you can remember."

"OK, sir." Detective Hall watched as chief Detective Mayfield walked out of his office and closed the door behind him. Detective Hall placed an ice pack on his head and closed his eyes.

Chapter Seventeen

Symone was sitting in her office watching the news when Slim Boogie walked in.

"I see you watching the news," said Slim Boogie.

"Yeah, I am. Red Invee's shooter missed last night," replied Symone. "Now that's just one more thing for District Attorney Kendrick to bring up in court," she added.

"Do you think it's going to fall back on you?"

"No, it shouldn't. There are no ties, but District Attorney Kendrick will paint a picture on how Detective Hall's attempted murder and my trial are connected to each other. But that's neither here nor there. How is the record label coming along?"

"Everything is how you want it. I just put everything on pause until your trial is over."

"I want everything on pause right now, everything, let Perk G know, whatever is not sold—pick it back up and put it in the new stash house. I want everything clean just in case they try to raid us again. Let Iceman and Pistol know, if they are under the age of twenty-one, I don't want them in the building. I want ID's checked thoroughly. All they need is one slip-up and we are fucked. I'm not stupid. I know the F.B.I is watching me, so I have to stay in the shadows at all times not only to protect myself but our family as well. Go tell Iceman and Pistol what I said as well as Perk G. Time is not on our side right now."

"OK. I'll go take care of that right now, Rose."

Symone reached into her bag and pulled out a *black and mild* and lit it.

"Also, let them know all books are closed, no new members are allowed in our family."

***

"Red Invee, we have a problem."

"I saw it on the news already, Tasha, he let one get away last night. We have to take a greater risk now and kill him in the open, where he feels he'll be safer. If we don't, it could cost us more in the long run. Tasha, how is Masi and Muscle doing on the project I put them on?"

"I know I saw them all going to *Passions* the other night."

"That's good. Make sure you tell them we need to know everything about him, from where his family lives to where he grew up."

"Jamila, you know they probably gave him a new identity."

"You know what, Tasha? I didn't think of that, still have them pull his bluff card, and I'll call Crystal and see what she can pull up on him for me. Until then keep your eyes open and ear to the ground. This is the second time I've dealt with the Feds and trust me, when they walk through the door they are going to have everything they need to build a case against us. Let me call Crystal and see what she can do for us."

Tasha nodded and walked out of the door.

***

Gino was in his backyard putting tomatoes in a basket as Joey stood guard.

"Gino, do you trust Vinnie?"

"How can I trust a man who set Alex up to be killed! Someone from his own family. I don't trust him. I don't respect him. He will always be a snake in my eyes. Joey, he came to my house telling me how Red Invee and Rose are going to be the downfall to the mob, but told Rose the Lenacci family will be there to help her if need be. He has something planned up his sleeve and I know it."

"So you want me to have someone keep an eye on him?"

"Yeah, do that, let's see what Mr. Lenacci has planned. Have the new boy go get the car ready, we are gonna pay Mrs. LaCross a visit, and Joey—if Vinnie is up to anything by going against my word, kill him, and hang his body over the Brooklyn Bridge."

Chapter Eighteen

Jamila walked into Panache Fine Jewelry. Muscle and Masi waited for her at the front door as she went to talk to Symone. When Symone came out of the back room and saw Jamila, she walked over and gave Jamila a hug and a kiss on the cheek.

"Hey, beautiful, how are you holding up?" Jamila asked.

"I'm good. The D.A. is painting a picture of me like I'm a mad dog."

"That's his job, to get a conviction by all means, but don't worry. His time is coming. Let me tell you something that our father used to always say to me: 'Adversity is another way to measure the greatness of individuals, there will never be a crisis in your life that doesn't make you stronger'. Rose, you are feared in New York City, everyone knows who you are. This case is bigger than Detective Boatman's murder. This case is about taking down a mafia family. I've been in your position before. The only difference is they had me dead to the wrong. Pictures of me standing over two dead bodies, gun in hand. The case they have against you is so weak I don't know how it made it this far, but we will talk about that later. I came to tell you that the F.B.I sent an undercover agent in my house, and nine times out of ten if they did that to me then they did it to you as well. So, watch who comes around you, and watch who your employees bring around."

"I will. So, what are you gonna do with the rat in your house?"

"Trap him, then kill him. Rose, listen to me, call a meeting, talk to your family, because there's a rat amongst you. Find him or her, set the trap and kill the beast."

"Jamila, thank you for everything."

"That's what I'm here for, Symone. I love you."

"I love you more."

"Alright, Symone, I have to go, I'll be in touch."

***

Saynomore

"Yo, this shit is crazy up in her, poppin' bottles and throwin' hunnids, big ballin' shit!" D.C. said as he was getting a lap dance and throwing back shots of Cîroc back to back.

"This is how we do, baby, we get the bread, fuck the baddest bitches, and drive the newest whips, we real live rock stars!" Masi said, bragging, taking a double shot of Cîroc.

"Baby girl, thanks for the lap dance. Here's a fifty, beautiful. I'll call you back in a few, let me holler at my two mans for a minute. Yo, Muscle, Masi, I fuck with you two niggas the long way, for the last few weeks y'all been showing a nigga much love. Drinks, parties, clubs, bitches, but we need to talk about this money, I have a few bands I'm trying to drop off on you two," D.C. told them.

Muscle took a shot of Cîroc and looked at Masi.

"How much bread you talking about?" Muscle asked.

"Two hundred grand."

"So you want five birds?"

"Big facts, Muscle."

"Where you gonna push that much weight off at?"

"I have a few homies, upstate New York, who be pushing my weight for me, Muscle."

Muscle took another shot of Cîroc.

"You know what? I like you, D.C., I'm going to give you my stamp. I think it's time you meet the Queen. What do you say, Masi?"

"Yeah, I'll take a shot to that shit, let him meet the Don hands down. Now come on, let's get some more bitches over here. I'm trying to fuck one of these hoes tonight."

Chapter Nineteen

Agent Brooks waited in an Old Mill Cadillac with Special Agent Carter.

"You know, Brooks, my great-grandfather used to work in this mill six days a week just to bring home two hundred and fifty dollars. If you was working here, then you were a breadwinner."

'I know, Carter, my father used to tell me the stories about the men that used to work here. He told me the explosion killed over forty men that fatal day. He would tell me at night you could still hear the men's cries."

"Yeah, Brooks, I've heard the stories. The closing of this mill was the downfall of this city, and the rise of drugs. So, tell me again how long your guy has been on this case, Brooks?"

"Eight weeks. He just told me last night they want him to spy on Jamila LaCross. Here he comes now pulling up."

Both agents watched as Corey stepped out of the car and walked towards them.

"Agent Corey, this is Special Agent Carter."

"How are you doing, sir?"

"Good. So, Brooks told me that you are doing a good job, a great job."

"I'm doing my best, sir. I just got two of her Lt's to agree on meeting Jamila LaCross on Friday."

"Do you know where that meeting is going to take place?"

"No, I do not know, sir."

Agent Carter looked at Brooks.

"What do you think of that, Brooks?"

"It's a hard choice, sir, how do you feel about that, Corey?"

"I'm going to do what I have to do to bring her down, sir."

"Brooks, are you going to put a wire on him?"

"I don't think that's a good idea, sir. They might pat him down. Remember Jamila has never been caught slipping. Corey's already walking into the devil's house. I don't want to put gas on his back."

"Brooks, I want eyes on him at all times; where he goes, they go."

Saynomore

"Corey, where do they think you hustle at?" asked Agent Brooks.

"I told them that I have a spot in upstate New York, sir."

"Brooks, you got him in, make sure you get him out. Corey, think fast, because you just got put in the belly of the beast."

Special Agent Carter patted Corey two times on the back before he walked back to his car.

"Sir, what was all that about?"

"Corey, we put two undercover agents into the LaCross family a few years back and one of them got out because it was too dangerous and a week later the other agent's body was found at a park in Long Island. After that no one would go undercover in the LaCross family again, so play your cards right because the wrong words could get you killed."

***

"Mr. Sabrano, the car is out front sir. Who do you want to go see first?" Joey asked.

"Take me to see Red Invee. I want to see how our Queen Don is doing with everything that's going on in the city." Gino Sabrano sat in the back of the limo, smoking a cigar as he looked out the window at the city of Queens. It took them twenty-five minutes to reach *Jelani's*.

"Joey, when we pull up, go inside and let them know I'm out here, and tell Red Invee to come take a ride with me."

"Yes, sir."

When the limo pulled up in front of *Jelani's*, Gino watched as his driver went inside to deliver his message. He sat quietly waiting for Jamila to come outside as he smoked his cigar. He saw Jamila come out a few minutes later, and his driver opened the limo door waiting for her to get in.

"Hello, Mr. Sabrano, how are you doing today?"

"I'm good, Red Invee," Mr. Sabrano said as he grabbed her hand and kissed it.

"So, Mr. Sabrano, what brings you by today?"

"A visitor, who came to my house, who I'm having a very hard time trusting after our conversation."

"And who was this visitor?"

"Vinnie Lenacci."

"And what did that fat boy have to say?"

"He said to me in so many words that you and Rose need to be killed before you bring down the ship with all of us on it."

"You know what? I should have killed his slimy ass the very first time he crossed me. I thought killing his daughter would teach him to stay in his place. Now I see I have to cut the head off the serpent."

Gino listened as he smoked his cigar, as the limo drove around the city of Queens.

"Jamila, you have become too powerful. In a way you are like the 'untouchable', a lot of families see this. In a way Vinnie is right about the feds' case against us. You brought back what the mafia had lost, the fear of the people, but with the positive comes the negative, and that is the fed cases. I stand on what I said and I told Vinnie that you are the best Don that came after me. Tony was some bullshit and so was Chris. You brought order back, but just like me Jamila, when things were getting too hot, I stepped down from that position, for my safety and the safety of the families."

"So you are telling me you want me to step down?"

"No, I'm telling you I want you to do what's best for everyone. Jamila, you have done something no black person has done before. You became the Don, you brought order back among the families, you won, you did it, what more do you want to accomplish?"

"Nothing, Mr. Sabrano. So if I step down, who becomes the next Don?"

"The families will vote and choose who they feel will be the best Don."

"So, what do I do about Vinnie's disloyalty?"

"As of right now, you are still the Queen Don, you make that choice." The limo came to a stop in front of *Jelani's*. Jamila leaned over and kissed Gino on the cheek.

"Gino, may I ask one favor from you."

Saynomore

"And what is that?"

"Call all the families from everywhere, and set up a meeting for me."

"I can do that for you, and I will let you know the day and time this meeting will take place."

Jamila opened up the limo door and stepped out. Gino watched as she walked back into *Jelani's*.

Chapter Twenty

"Detective Hall, it's been a few days since the attack at your house. I just got back from seeing Amber from C.S.I, and she told me whoever was in your house was professional. He didn't leave any fingerprints at all. His bullet casings were clean. There was no sign of breaking or entering. Detective Hall, God was on your side."

Detective Hall didn't say a word, as he sat in lead Detective Mayfield's office drinking a cup of coffee.

"For the next few weeks I'm gonna keep a squad car outside of your house."

"Sir, we both know that Symone Rose is behind this, or her sister Jamila LaCross."

"Hall, it's not what we know, but what we can prove. Detective, you did what a lot of officers have swept under the rug. You came forth with the information that you found, and this is the backlash of it all, and I can tell you a lot more is going to come out of this trial before it is all over."

"Sir, I have a house in Queensbridge that I can stay in for now. I'm not going back to my house until this trial is over."

"So, I'll cancel the patrol car, but do you mind if we put someone in your house to set up a trap for this son of a bitch?"

"Do what you have to do, because the next time I see him, when you come to the scene, you will be looking at a dead body."

Detective Mayfield leaned back in his seat and took a sip of his coffee as he watched Detective Hall get up and walk out of his office, closing the door behind him.

***

Pistol pulled up outside off of Lincoln Ave. in his all-black BMW. He was smoking a blunt as he waited for Kia to come out of the projects. He turned the radio up as he listened to 50 Cent's 'Many Men'. He looked up and saw Kia walking out of the projects to his car. She was looking real good to him, with her windbreaker outfit on. He smiled at her as she opened up the car door to get in.

Saynomore

"What's up, beautiful?"
"Nothing, I see you on time."
"For you, I will never be late."
"I hear you, Pistol, so, where are you taking me?"
"Does it matter?"
"No."
"So then enjoy the ride, baby girl. You smoke?"
"No, I don't."
"Well, today you do. Enjoy the ride and hit this gas."
Kia sat back and looked around as Pistol drove through the city.
"This is a nice car."
"Thanks, it was a gift."
"From who? I need a friend like that."
"Rose, she takes care of her family."
"I have been watching her trial on TV. They have nothing on her."
Pistol looked at her but didn't say anything as he passed her the blunt. Kia took two puffs of the blunt and passed it back.
"Kia, check me out, I have to go by the casino, so while I take care of my business, you can gamble or play the slot machines. I shouldn't be long."
"'I got you, babe, you know where to find me, when you finish taking care of your business."
"That's why I'm rockin' with you, Queen."
Kia smiled and reached and grabbed his hand as he was driving.

***

Kevin took his glasses off and rubbed his eyes as he laid them on his desk. He put his glasses back on as he continued to read over Symone Rose's file. A knock at the door took his attention off of the file that he was reading.
"Come in."
That's when Katrina walked into the office.
"Hey, my apologies, I thought Kendrick was in here."
"No, he had something he had to take care of. Katrina, right?"

"Yes."

Kevin got up and shook her hand.

"So, how is the chase going?" Katrina asked.

"I live in the real world, Katrina, we're not gonna win. All Kendrick did was make her feel even more untouchable. I read over the last few years all the killings in Queens, New York and in Brooklyn, New York. When Jamila was in prison for five years, Symone had Queens. When Jamila was released, Symone was already in Brooklyn. Like patterns, Katrina, the same way the murders happened in Queens, starting in Brooklyn, everything was just swept under the rug, and all that tells me is that this is bigger than two sisters. They have real political protection from the city, cops, D.A.'s, judges, politicians. Even if we did have Symone dead to the wrong, she would get off. Jamila was standing over two dead bodies, gun in hand, dead to the wrong, with video footage of her killing those two men, and she only gets five years? John Gotti was standing next to one dead body and got life in prison."

"I'm glad you see the picture I've been trying to paint for Kendrick. The question is, what are you going to do about it now?"

"That's a good question. What do you think I should do?"

Katrina turned around and walked towards the door. She stopped and looked at Kevin before opening the door.

"Walk away, before you become more involved than you want to be."

Kevin watched as she walked out the door, closing it behind her.

***

"Pistol, this place is fly as hell. I didn't know it was like this up in here."

"Yeah, Rose be wanting the best of the best of shit. Check me out, Kia, remember what I told you, I got some business to take care of, so I'll be gone for a few." Pistol reached into his pockets and pulled out a stack of hundreds, and peeled off twenty and gave them to Kia.

"Here's two thousand. I'll be back in a few. I have to go."
"Thanks, Pistol."
"No problem, beautiful."

Kia watched as Pistol walked off and disappeared through the back doors.

Symone watched from the security cameras as Pistol made his way upstairs.

"Iceman, come here for a second."
"What's up, Rose?"
"Who is this female? Do you see her? Pistol just brought her here."
"I don't know. I never seen her before."
"OK. Come on, let's get ready to have this meeting."

Symone walked and took her seat at the head of the table.
"Pistol, you are late."
"My apologies, Ms. Rose."
"Come take your seat. Now that everyone is here, Perk G, how much product do you have left?"
"Twenty kilos on the head."
"Who at this table still got work that they haven't got off yet?"
"I have two kilos still put up, Rose."
"When do you think you will be able to get them off, Iceman?"
"If not this week, then definitely next week for sure."
"Who else has any more work?"
"I have about one left, but I should have it sold by the end of the week."
"OK. Pistol, do that. What about you, Halo?"
"I have nothing left."
"And you Slim Boogie?"
"Probably under a quarter."
"Perk G, what was the gross income from the last shipment?"
"A little over five million, Rose."
"I know I told Slim to tell you all to put everything up just in case they raid us again, but I've changed my mind, we have to keep a grip on Brooklyn. Perk G, give Slim and Halo five kilos each, and the same thing for Iceman and Halo."

"I'll do that as soon as I get to the stash, Rose."

Rose stood up and walked around the table looking at everyone. She stopped and put her hands on Pistol's shoulders and started rubbing them.

"Pistol, who is that female that you brought here."

"Just a female I met a few weeks ago. She's nobody."

"You know the feds will send a female to fuck you and suck your dick and even tell you they love you. Pistol, if she's not who she says she is, I'm going to kill her and I'm going to kill you." Symone gave Pistol a kiss on the cheek before walking off.

"I told Slim Boogie to tell all of you the books are closed. No new members. Everyone here, the work that you are about to receive, I need you all to get off faster, so if you have to put in twice the effort to do that, get it done. Perk G, it's time for you to get your hands dirty. I have a friend in the District Attorney's office who is very loyal and reliable. She informed me that District Attorney Kendrick has a friend, who is helping him against me on this trial. I told her to try and get him to walk away, but he refused, so now he's involved. Red Invee told me she got this, but we put our own work in as well. This is what I want you to do: Kidnap this new Assistant District Attorney's—Kevin's—two daughters and bring them to the white house. I don't want no harm to come to them, not one hair on their head touched, do I make myself clear?"

"As water," Perk G replied.

"Make sure there is food, video games, and whatever else that is needed to make them comfortable. Iceman, I want you to shoot up District Attorney Kendrick's house, one hundred rounds, burn the car afterwards. Don't nobody reach out to me. Talk to Halo and he will talk to me. Move smart because we are under investigation, and I am blazing hot right now. Does anyone at this table have anything to say?"

Pistol raised his hand.

"Symone, I would never put this family in jeopardy, or disrespect you."

"Pistol, you've disrespected me twice today, as well as put this family in jeopardy. You brought a female to our place of business

Saynomore

knowing you had a meeting to attend, then you showed up to the meeting late, and why is this? Because you let a female distract you from me. Point one, you brought a female with you. Point two, you were late. Perk G, get them the product and then get the job done as soon as possible. I have nothing more to say. Pistol, remember what I said."

Symone got up and walked out the back door.

Chapter Twenty-One

Gino Sabrano stood up and looked around at everyone in the room.

"I would like to thank all of you for coming out here today. This is a meeting that should have taken place years ago. It's a new day and a new time. There has been more blood spilled on the streets of New York in history. It's not like the old days, but this meeting was called here today to get an understanding against all of us. For those of you who don't know, this is Jamila LaCross, the Queen Don. You know the name, I speak to the families from California, Las Vegas, and Chicago, now you see her face. It's because of her we are feared again. She has brought order back. She has helped us grow economically in the drug trade also."

"Mr. Sabrano, if I may."

"The table is yours, Mr. Savato."

"Thank you, Mr. Sabrano. My family heard about the LaCross family. I don't know, ten years ago, after a good friend of mine was killed by her hands. Tony Lenacci. From the understanding we got, she was just knocking off bosses so she could rise to the top, and the families in New York City was letting it happen, then it came across my desk that she became the Queen Don. After that, I cut off all contact with the families in New York City. A negro over an Italian, unheard of."

"Mr. Savato, there is much more to that story. Tony was extorting the families in New York City. Tony Lenacci drew first blood, and it cost him his life and the lives of several of his family members. But to make a long story short, she wouldn't back down from Tony or his family when the gun fire began. Who do you think is selling us cocaine for fifteen thousand a kilo? Or whose judges and District Attorneys are keeping us out of prison? Or who killed Deniro when he was ready to rat on all of us? Who do you think save most of the families here when Sammy set us up in the train yard? But we are not here for a history lesson, we are here for the continuation of the mafia, that is first and foremost."

Jamila sat quietly, she and Tasha, as Mr. Sabrano spoke.

"I'm going to let Mrs. LaCross speak."

Saynomore

Jamila stood up. "Thank you, Mr. Sabrano. I would like to thank all of the families here for coming to this meeting at my invitation, but I did not call this meeting to get anybody's approval of me. I called this meeting to announce to all of the families that I'm stepping down as Queen Don. I feel that it isn't in my best interests to continue on as Queen Don. I did all I could do to help every family that came to me, but with the trial of Rose for the murder of Detective Boatman, it's bringing too much heat to me and my family and the Rose family, and I don't want any other family to be put under investigation. Now let me clarify this—whoever takes my position as head don, understand you will have to make the same sacrifices I made. I will not hand over anything to you. You will show the families here today that you are the right person for this position. I have been shot, been in wars, and I've killed law enforcement men and women, I have killed the innocent to make my point clear. There is a special place in hell just for me."

"Excuse me, Mrs. LaCross, if I may."

"The table is yours, Mr. Gambino."

"I have witnessed Red Invee's rise from the very beginning. Frankie Landon vouched for her. She may be black, but she is as true and loyal as one of us. She has never gone against her word during the time she has been our Don. There has never been more order among us. We are on the top. We control the streets again. The flow of cocaine has never been more plentiful. Who at this table can say they can fill her shoes, take her place. I don't want you to step down, Red Invee. Everything that comes your way, we should all face it together, since you've carried all of us on our back. The families need to show you the same loyalty."

"If I may, Mr. Gambino."

"Mr. Scott, the table is yours."

"Mr. Gambino is right. We all need to stand behind the Queen Don."

Gino Sabrano looked at Jamila and then at everyone else as Mr. Scott was talking. Gino Sabrano leaned over and whispered in Jamila's ear.

"You are truly the Don they chose."

Mr. Scott took his seat and Gino stood up.

"Does anyone here oppose that Red Invee should not continue as the Queen Don, speak up."

No one said a word.

"Gino, I sat here the whole time just listening. I agree with Mr. Savato, only Italians should be the Don and I vote for myself to be the head Don here today."

"Vinnie, your family had the seat and did nothing, nothing came out of it, but dues and wars. Why should you hold the position as the new Don?"

"Because I know what comes with that position, Mr. Sabrano."

"But what will you bring to the table? Betrayal, treachery, treason?"

"How dare you insult me like that, Mr. Sabrano!"

"It's no secret that you had Alex killed for the position you hold now."

"I did what I had to do for the survival of my family."

Jamila stood up. "Enough, there will not be any more head Dons. At all. Everything will be voted on from here on out. Gino Sabrano will be the voice of reason for all of us. Everyone here will honor each other's blocks and areas. If you agree to what I'm proposing, raise your hand in my favor."

One by one everyone raised their hands.

"There is nothing more to talk about then, the votes are in, there will be no more head Dons. I thank all the families for coming here today."

Gino Sabrano gave Jamila a hug and a kiss on the left cheek.

"Once again you brought order to the table, Jamila."

"No, once again we brought order to the table, Mr. Sabrano."

Tasha watched Jamila kiss Gino on the cheek once again before walking away.

Saynomore

Chapter Twenty-Two

"Kendrick, with two more weeks left in this trial, what do you feel is going to happen? Are they going to find her guilty?" Jessica asked.

"I don't know, Jessica," Kendrick said as she lay in his arms in the comfort of their bed.

"I have a feeling that the judge has already been paid off, members of the jury as well. I'm fighting a losing battle."

"What about the witness you have?"

"She was really a scare tactic," Kendrick told Jessica.

"That's not going to work. Her alibi isn't worth two pennies."

"So what now?" Jessica asked.

"I can try and tell the best story I can to the people."

"What are they doing about Chief Tadem being killed at the other house? They have to know that Symone Rose or Jamila La-Cross is responsible for it, right?"

"That's the thing, it's not what you know, it's what you can prove." At that point Kendrick grabbed Jessica and rolled off of the bed onto the floor and laid on top of her, shielding her with his body as their house was being shot up. Bullets ripped through the walls of the house and broke windows. The sound of bullets echoing through the house rang for three minutes non-stop.

"Baby, are you OK?"

"Yes, yes. Oh my God! Someone just shot up our house."

"Stay down, don't move, let me check to see if they are gone."

"No, don't leave me."

"Jessica, stay down, I will be right back. Here, take the phone and call the police. Now." Kendrick looked out the window and saw tail lights turning the corner.

***

Breaking news flashed across the TV screen as head detective Mayfield watched the news cast from his living room couch.

"This is Barbara Smith with Channel Five Action News. Last night the house of District Attorney Kendrick, who is prosecuting the notorious Symone Rose for the murder of Detective Deontay Boatman, was shot up between the hours of eleven p.m. and twelve a.m. But this is not the first incident since the trials began not even two months ago. Chief Anthony Tadem of the Twenty-sixth police precinct was found murdered inside the shed of District Attorney Kendrick's backyard. As of right now the District Attorney has twenty-four-hour security until this trial is over."

Detective Mayfield cut the TV off, he got his coat off of the coat rack, picked up his keys off the bookshelf in the living room and walked out the front door.

***

"Kendrick, I know how bad you want to put a nail in this bitch, but don't let this case cost you your life."

"I'm fine. It's not going to cost me my life. Come on, let's get ready for this trial. We got thirty minutes."

As they walked into the courtroom, Kendrick looked at Symone sitting next to her two attorneys. It took everything in him not to say anything to her. Then the bailiff entered and spoke.

"All rise for the honorable Judge Mills." Everyone stood.

"The prosecutor may call his first witness."

District Attorney Kendrick stood up.

"I call Ms. Cindy Morris to the stand."

Symone watched as Cindy Morris walked to the witness stand.

"Would you state your name for the court please?"

"Yes, my name is Cindy Morris."

"Thank you, and can you tell us where you were working the night that you witnessed Detective Deontay Boatman's murder?"

"I was working at Creams Sports Bar in the Bronx."

"Can you tell us what you saw that night?"

"Yes, I can. I went outside to smoke a cigarette, and saw a woman walking up the block very fast. She had a gun in her hand. I watched as she said something to Detective Boatman, then she shot him. I watched as the fire sparked from the gun, and a few seconds later she poured something on him and struck a match, then I saw the flames. Then she took off down the block. When she got to the corner, she tried to stop another car. When the car stopped, she shot an old lady that was driving the car, and jumped in and drove off."

"Ms. Morris, can you point to who did all of this on the said night and time of Detective Boatman's murder?"

"Yes, she is sitting right over there with her two lawyers."

"OK. Thank you, Ms. Morris." District Attorney Kendrick concluded.

"Your witness, Attorney Foster," said Judge Mills.

"Thank you, Your Honor. Ms. Morris, the night you allegedly witnessed the killing of Detective Boatman, were you on any drugs?"

"Yes, I was."

"And would you please tell the court what drug you were on that night?"

Cindy lowered her head and spoke softly.

"Cocaine."

"Thank you, and were you under the influence of alcohol as well?"

"Yes, I was."

"How many drinks would you say you'd had?"

"I don't know, a few, I had been drinking all night."

"So how can you say that you saw Symone Rose that night if you were on a street drug and under the influence of alcohol?"

"From a distance it looked like her."

"Hold up, you said it looked like her, have you ever seen Symone Rose before the night of the murder?"

"Only on TV once."

"So you never saw her before, but you just knew it was her the night that Detective Boatman was killed? Ms. Morris, I have one more question for you, have you ever been arrested before?"

"Objective, Your Honor."

"Overruled. Answer the question, Miss. Morris!" stated Judge Mills.

"Yes, I have been arrested before."

Saynomore

"And for what, may I ask?"

Again, Cindy lowered her head and spoke softly.

"Prostitution."

"Thank you, Ms. Morris. Your Honor, that will be all."

"The court will take a thirty minutes' recess."

Assistant District Attorney Kevin leaned over and whispered into Kendrick's ear.

"I have to make a phone call. My phone has been going off every five minutes."

"OK. I'll be right out there, right after I talk with Symone's attorneys."

Kevin got up and walked out the courtroom.

"Kendrick, drop the case, you are not going to win."

"Alexander, I did not hear a fat bitch sing yet."

Attorney Foster smiled and patted Kendrick on the back.

"She will be singing soon," he told him as he walked away.

Kendrick walked out the courtroom to see Kevin running out the front doors to the courthouse. Katrina walked up next to him.

"What's going on? Where is Kevin going?" Kendrick asked.

"You don't know? Well, let me be the first to tell you. Congratulations, you dragged him into this bullshit and his two daughters were kidnapped this morning and his wife was tied up."

Kendrick looked at Katrina as she walked away. Alexander Foster was standing behind Kendrick when Katrina told him what happened. He looked at Symone as she walked out the courtroom and knew she was the monster that Kendrick painted her out to be. Attorney Foster walked off. Kendrick saw Symone coming out of the courtroom; he looked at her and she winked at him. He was in disbelief all this was happening to him. Looking at his watch, he saw he only had fifteen minutes before he had to go back into the courtroom. As he walked into the bathroom, he looked at himself in the mirror thinking about all the events that happened during this case. He ran the cold water and splashed some on his face. When he walked back into the courtroom, he looked at everyone sitting around, and then he took his seat.

"All rise for the Honorable Judge Mills," said the bailiff.

"You may all be seated," Judge Mills told the court.

"Your Honor, may I approach the bench?" asked District Attorney Kendrick.

"Yes, you may."

"I would like for a three-day recess."

"Hold on, counselor, approach the bench."

"Yes, Your Honor," Attorney Foster said as he got up from the defense table.

"The District Attorney's office is asking for a three-day recess. Do you agree with this?"

"Yes. I do, Your Honor."

"OK. Then we will start this trial back up in three days. Attention in the court, this trial will start again in three days on Wednesday the 19th."

"Mr. Foster, why is the trial being postponed for three days?" Symone asked her chief attorney.

"The District Attorney's office asked for it, but don't worry. Everything is in our favor."

Symone looked at District Attorney Kendrick as he ran out of the courtroom.

Saynomore

Chapter Twenty-Three

Symone waved at the crowd of people that were standing outside the courthouse. Once inside the limo, her phone went off.
"Hello."
"It's done." Then the phone went dead
"Driver, take me to Panache Fine Jewelry please."

***

Hampton Hill had a crowd of people around as the police had yellow caution tape, as Kendrick pulled up. He jumped out the car and ran to Kevin and his wife.
"Kevin, what happened?"
When Kevin turned around and looked at Kendrick, his eyes were bloodshot.
"My girls were kidnapped because of you and this case. I should have walked away at the very first sign I saw. Kendrick, stay the fuck away from me. The next time I see you, I will kill you, I swear to God." Kevin turned around and walked back to his wife.
Kendrick walked up to Detective Mayfield.
"What happened out here, Detective?"
"This morning around eight a.m. someone kicked in the door at gunpoint and tied up the wife and took the two girls and left this note."
Detective Mayfield held up the note in a plastic bag.
'*Kendrick bullshit just became your bullshit.*'
"Did anybody see anything?"
"Not one person at all. Kendrick, let me tell you something, you took on the mob, you took on Red Invee's kid sister. Did you really think this was going to be a piece of cake? A walk in the park? Chief Tadem is dead, your house has been shot up and now your friend's children have been kidnapped. If you could find her guilty, this case would be the highlight of your career, but you also have to ask yourself, at what cost is it worth it?" Detective Mayfield walked away from Kendrick after asking him that last question.

Saynomore

***

"You ready, baby boy? You ready to see the Queen?"

"Yeah, I'm ready, Muscle."

"Good, now let me tell you straight cakes, watch what you say because the wrong shit could get you killed, and if she tells me or Masi to pop your top, nigga, we going to pop the top and pour the drink."

D.C. nodded as they pulled up to *Jelani's*. When they walked in, the place was empty except for the guards that she had there with her.

He looked and saw Red Invee sitting at the back table by herself.

"You ready, D.C.?"

"Yeah."

"Hold up," one of the guards said. "Lift your arm up, you know the deal, pat down."

Jamila watched as they patted D.C. down and took his gun off of him.

"You will get this back when you leave," the guard said as he walked away.

"Come on, D.C., let's go see the Queen."

"Masi, Muscle, this must be D.C. you were telling me about."

"Yes, it's him, Mrs. LaCross."

"Hello, D.C."

"How are you doing, Mrs. LaCross?"

"I'm doing fine, please have a seat. Now, Masi told me you have your own operation in upstate New York."

"Yeah, I got a little something going on up there, nothing too big."

"So, I'm guessing you want to expand?"

"Yeah, that sounds about right."

"Muscle, go get me a bottle of Cîroc and two shot glasses. What type of numbers are we talking, D.C.?"

"Two hundred grand, what would that bring me?"

"I'll give you each one for twenty-four grand, so that will be eight of them, how does that sound to you?"

"That sounds good to me."

Muscle came back to the table with the bottle of Cîroc and poured two shots, one for Jamila and the other for D.C.

"Thank you, Muscle. Now here is our only problem. I need to know if I can trust you, D.C. and having a drink or going to a strip club isn't going to do it. I'm going to need you to get your hands dirty for me. I have a little problem I need taken care of. You do this for me and the door will be open for you to come into my house."

"What do you need for me to do?"

"Just stay ready. When I call, don't let me down. Do I make myself clear?"

"As water."

"Good. Now that we got the business out of the way, tell me, where are you from?"

"Syracuse, New York."

"I know they do a lot of killing in Syracuse, New York, but I didn't know they was getting money up there."

"Yeah, we got a cash flow."

"Come, take another shot with me and I will be in touch with you real soon, D.C." Jamila poured them both another shot, D.C. looked at her.

"To a new beginning."

"To a new beginning," Jamila replied. They tapped glasses and took their shots together.

Saynomore

Chapter Twenty-Four

Kendrick sat at his desk reading unsolved cases in Brooklyn and Queens. When Katrina walked into his office, he just looked up at her.

"Kendrick, I know how bad you want her, but look at what it's costing you. Now you have your childhood friend involved and look at what it just cost him. His two daughters. Let this case go, and put all your efforts into trying to help get Kevin's girls back."

Kendrick took his glasses off and put them on his desk.

"Katrina, I don't know what to do. This case is blowing up in my face every day."

"You have to weigh your cons and your pros, but this is what I want you to think about: Chief Tadem didn't push Cindy's statements, because everything she admitted to on record, he knew it wouldn't hold up in court. Detective Hall is on leave right now because he was about to have a face to face with Chief Tadem. Cindy's life will never be the same, she will forever have to look over her shoulder, and you should be lucky that one of those bullets didn't rip through your chest."

"You know what? You are right, I'm going to dismiss all charges against Symone Rose and see how the investigation is going to find Kevin's girls."

"Come on, I'll give you a hand on trying to find them. Now you're thinking, Kendrick."

***

"Tasha, I need you to handle something for me," Jamila said as she looked out her office window.

"Whatever you need me to do, I'll handle it."

"What's my number one rule? The first time you fuck up, you die. Young Cap is a liability. I want you to kill him. I reached out to him already. He's going to meet you at Hyde Park tomorrow night at nine. Don't do too much talking, just get the job done. When dealing with someone like Cap, headshots are the best. Don't underestimate him. He's good, real good." Jamila turned around and looked at Tasha.

'You don't have to worry about that. I don't fuck up. Three shots to the head and his fat ass is dead."

"And that's why I put my trust in you, beautiful."

"Jamila, I haven't been keeping up with the trial. How is it going?"

"One of my sources told me that the District Attorney is going to dismiss all charges against Symone ever since his friend's girls came up missing."

Tasha looked at Jamila with a smirk on her face.

"I know that look, Tasha, I swear I didn't have anything to do with it."

"I believe you, Queen, I'm going to go get ready to rock Cap to sleep."

Jamila smiled.

"Tasha, yeah, in my Keisha voice—'Rock-a-bye-baby'."

Tasha laughed as she was walking out the door.

***

"Gino, a lot of the families are pleased about Red Invee's decision about voting on everything from here on out."

"Yeah, all but one. The Lenacci family, I saw it all over Vinnie's face," Gino said as he watched the news about the two girls who'd been kidnapped.

"Vinnie is going to try something, in his eyes, he's got a point to prove."

"You really think he's going to try something?"

"Yeah, I do, but this time he's going to be the one laying in a pool of blood. I'm going to make sure of it myself."

"And what about Red Invee?"

"Red Invee is going to keep her grip on Queens, but stepping down as the Queen Don is a lot of weight off her shoulders. Now she will have to run her family and to work on her ins and outs, but as of right now our focus needs to be on Vinnie. He believes that in his heart he has something to prove."

Gino walked to the car alongside his bodyguard–Joey. When Joey went to open the car door, Gino stopped him.

"Wait, Joey, didn't it rain last night?"

"Yeah, it did."

"So why is the door handle dry? And the footprints around the car. Step back from the car, Joey."

As both of them stepped back, Gino took the car keys from Joey. When they were far enough back, Gino pressed the car alarm to unlock the doors and the car exploded. Both men jumped back and looked at each other.

'You were right, Gino, Vinnie did have a trick up his sleeve."

"Yeah, he did. He must have thought that I was getting comfortable in the hills. Now it's my turn to pull a trick out of my hat."

Saynomore

Chapter Twenty-Five

Young Cap stood quietly with two .357's in his hands, looking at Tasha's car when it pulled up. He stepped off the porch and walked around the house before Tasha got out of the car. Tasha stepped out of her car and looked around as she followed Young Cap. She walked into the garage where he was cleaning his guns.

"Let me guess, Red Invee wants to know what happened from the source? That's why your here?"

"If you know that, then that means I don't have to ask."

Tasha leaned against the door frame and folded her arms against her chest. Young Cap looked at her with a crooked smile. He hated being questioned.

"He came in the house, I knocked him down, he was quick on his feet jumping back up. I shot him two times in the chest, he had his vest on, but made it out the front door. I shot his car up but he had a guardian angel by his side. Afterward, I walked back into his house, I picked up his bag and left, it's right over there to the left."

Tasha looked at the bag sitting on the floor.

"So, when will you be getting the job done?"

"As soon as I locate him. I've been watching the house for the last two weeks and he hasn't been there."

"Well, I have another message from Jamila."

Young Cap turned his head when Tasha told him that he wasn't paying her any attention as he continued to clean his guns.

"And what's the message?" he asked, never looking back at Tasha.

Tasha pulled her black .9mm out.

"Rock-a-bye-baby." When Young Cap looked up, she was already letting off shots to his face. Young Cap's face hit the table he'd been cleaning his guns on. Blood poured out his head as he lay there eyes open. Dead. Tasha walked over, picked up the black duffle bag and made her way back to her car.

***

Saynomore

Symone sat at her table reading the newspaper article about Assistant District Attorney Kevin's missing daughters. It hadn't been forty-eight hours yet. There was an Amber alert on the news, pictures of the house they were taken from with pictures of both the girls that were taken. There was a knock at the door.

"Come in."

"Ms. Rose, you have a visitor."

"Who came to see me?"

"Pastor Rose."

"And what does the good man of God want?"

"I don't know. He wouldn't say."

"Let's see what Pastor Rose has to say, bring him in."

Symone watched as Pastor Rose walked inside her office.

"Hello, Pastor, how are you?"

"I'm fine, thank you for seeing me."

"Always, Pastor, what can I do for you?"

Pastor Rose looked up at Halo then back at Symone; she knew he wanted to talk in private. Symone waved Halo off, and once the door was closed she said:

"You can talk now, Pastor."

"Ms. Rose, District Attorney Kendrick came to see me yesterday and told me to tell you all charges against you will be dropped and he will never try to prosecute you again if you will return the girls."

Symone looked at Pastor Rose.

"Pastor, don't take this the wrong way, I have a lot of respect for you."

"Take what the wrong way?"

Symone picked up the phone and called Halo back into her office. Pastor Rose looked when Halo walked back in.

"Halo, search Pastor Rose to make sure he doesn't have on a wire please. Pastor, do you mind standing up please so Halo can search you."

Symone waited as Halo patted down Pastor Rose for a wire.

"He's clean, Ms. Rose."

"OK. Thank you, Halo."

"Sorry about that, Pastor, but I had to be sure you are clean, because of the question you asked me. Here's the deal: I want all charges dropped against me and my family as well as the LaCross family, and I will see what I can do about getting the girls back for him."

"I will let him know, Ms. Rose." Pastor Rose got up and walked to the door, then stopped and turned around.

"Ms. Rose, the girls will be alive, right?"

"There will be no harm done to them, I promise."

Pastor Rose opened up the door and walked out. Symone opened up her Gucci bag and pulled out a *black and mild* and lit it, and then she picked back up the paper.

Tasha walked into Jamila's office with the duffle bag over her shoulders.

"How did it go?"

"He told me what happened. I told him I have a message from you. By the time he looked up, he was dead. Rock-a-bye-baby. This is the bag he took from Detective Hall's house."

"Let's see what our good detective has in his bag, shall we?"

Tasha brought Jamila the bag and put it on the table. Tasha watched as Jamila opened the bag. Jamila pulled out a video camera, a tape recorder, two folders full with files, a police jacket and a pair of gloves. Jamila hooked the video camera up to her laptop and pressed play. Her and Tasha watched footage of Symone throwing a fair at one of the projects in Brooklyn, and video footage of Judge Mills taking money from Halo, then the tape came to a stop. She pressed play on the recorder and it was a conversation with him and Judge Mills about Symone Rose, talking about the money. Judge Mills was going to cross Symone out. Jamila stopped the recording. "Symone needs to be glad Young Cap got this before the police. Take this to Symone and let her deal with it." Jamila placed everything back in the bag and Tasha walked out.

Saynomore

Chapter Twenty-Six

Vinnie rode down the parkway in the back of the limo, smoking a cigar, headed to New Jersey.

"Vinnie, I just got word that the bomb went off and Gino is dead as of yesterday morning."

"Who told you that?"

"Walter from the Gambino family told me. They plan on having his service one day this week."

"Do they have any idea who did it?"

"Not a clue."

"Then you know what, Bull? That sounds like a win-win for us."

"So why are we headed out to New Jersey?"

"I got a call from Silvio Milano today telling me he needs to talk to me about some new business, but not over the phone. Now with Gino out of the way we can move like we want to, and right after his funeral we make sure Red Invee has one. Don't you just love when a plan comes together?"

After going through the tollbooth, they made the right off the first exit and stopped at the red light at the corner of the intersection. A black hummer pulled up on the side of them. When the light turned green and the limo pulled off, a blue van smacked the front of the limo head on. Two men jumped out with AR 15's and started shooting up the right side of the limo. The only thing that could be heard was gunshots. The Hummer door opened up and a man in a black suit stepped out of the Hummer and threw hand grenades into the limo's broken windows. He gave the two men with the AR 15's the thumbs up and got in the hummer and pulled off. The other two men jumped back into the van and as they were driving off they saw the limo explode and burst into flames. The man in the Hummer pulled out his phone and called Gino. After two rings, Gino picked up.

"It's done."

Those were the only words Gino heard before the line went dead.

Saynomore

***

"All rise for the Honorable Judge Mills."

"Thank you. You may all be seated."

"Your Honor, may the counselor for the defense and I approach the bench?"

"Yes, you may. What is the meaning of this, District Attorney Kendrick?"

"The prosecutor's office is dropping all charges against Symone Rose."

"Are you sure?"

"Yes, Your Honor."

"Very well, then go back to your seats."

"Ladies and Gentlemen of the court, this case has been dismissed."

District Attorney Kendrick looked at Symone, and she winked at him. Symone stood up and gave both her attorneys a hug and smiled as she walked out the courtroom.

"Ms. Rose, do you have anything to say for the camera?"

"Yes, I do. I'm glad justice came out in the courtroom today. Now I don't have to look back. I can move forward with my life. I also would like to thank everyone who supported me during this three-week trial. Your love and support meant a lot to me, thank you again."

"Ms. Rose, I have one question, how do you feel about the rumors that you have your hands in the abduction of Assistant District Attorney Kevin's daughters?"

"All I can say is my sympathy goes out to the families and their children are in my prayers, and I pray that their children are returned safely. That's all I have to say. Thank you."

Symone made her way to the limo that was outside waiting for her. Halo opened the door for her as she walked up to the limo to get in.

"How do you feel now that the trial is over?"

"Relieved, very relieved."

"So, where do we go from here?"

"Home and we start moving a lot smarter, but I still want that rat killed."

"What about the white house?"

"Give it two weeks at the most."

***

Gino walked into his back yard and looked at the view of the mountains and many trees surrounding them.

"Joey, you know why I like this view so much?"

"No. Why, boss?"

"Because from right here it looks so peaceful."

"I can understand why you like it here then."

"I just finished watching the news. Symone's trial is over and Vinnie is dead. They said his body was unrecognizable."

"That's good then, and I knew Symone would come out on top."

"Do you think anything is going to come back on us?"

"Not at all, but I do wonder who Vinnie told about the hit on me, or did he keep that under the rug? Knowing who he was dealing with he wouldn't want that to get out at all, so I'm sure just him and one other person knew about this, that's all. Joey, there are going to be many questions asked about the assassination of Vinnie, but hey, let them ask. Now, come on, let's take a hike into the woods, let me see if an old man can still make that walk."

As they walked through the hills, Gino had a stick in his hand to help his balance.

"How you feeling, Gino?"

"Like I need to take a break, Joey."

Gino leaned his back up against a tree as he was catching his breath. Joey looked around at all the trees as he walked back down to Gino. Once he got back to Gino, Joey asked

"How you feeling? Are you okay?"

"Yeah, I just needed to catch my breath. Come, give me a hand up, Joey."

Saynomore

As Joey walked up to Gino, Gino grabbed his hand and with the other hand he pulled his gun out and put it to Joey's stomach.

"You didn't think I'd figure it out? It was only a matter of time, Joey, and you dropped the ball."

Gino shot Joey three times in the stomach and he watched Joey hit the ground.

"You left breadcrumbs and I followed them, now look at you."

Gino pointed the gun at Joey's head and with the pull of the trigger Joey was dead. Gino turned around and walked back down the hill.

Chapter Twenty-Seven

"It's been weeks, Pastor, since I've had all charges against Symone dropped. Why haven't the girls showed up yet?"

"District Attorney Kendrick, we all know Ms. Rose to be a lady of her word."

"No, Pastor Rose, we know Rose to be a murderer, a killer, a drug dealer. She's no better than John Gotti, Tony Lenacci and the rest of those thugs." District Attorney Kendrick walked to his office window.

"Pastor, this city is so big, those girls could be anywhere," Kendrick said in a low, hurtful tone.

"I did this. I pulled Kevin and his family into this bullshit." District Attorney Kendrick lowered his head. Pastor Rose walked over to him and patted him on the back.

"Have faith in God, trust in his word." Pastor Rose turned around and walked out of District Attorney Kendrick's office.

***

Symone sat in the back seat of the BMW and watched from the corner as both girls held hands walking down the block to their house. For the past four weeks both girls had everything they could ever want, from dollhouses to play with to video games. Symone had set it up so the girls would think they were at Mickey Mouse Play House. When they knocked on the front door, their mother opened the door.

"Oh, my God, mommy! Both girls ran and hugged their mother, as she dropped to her knees crying as she held them.

"Baby, what's going on out here?" Kevin said as he ran downstairs. He stopped in his tracks when he saw his wife holding both girls in her arms.

"Daddy, daddy, I missed you," his youngest daughter said as she ran and jumped into his arms.

"I'm so happy you are home. I missed you so much. Where were you?"

"At Mickey Mouse Play House. He gave us cake and ice cream. We played games and ate pizza. There was a puppy there we played with too."

Kevin looked at his wife as his daughter was talking. His wife looked back at him as she got up and closed the front door. Symone was in the BMW watching everything.

"Come on, let's go. They're back home safely in their parents' arms."

Kevin looked out the window as the black BMW pulled off. Thirty minutes later there were three police cars and Detective Mayfield at Kevin's house writing out a police report.

"So let me get this right, Mrs. Long, you were in the kitchen and you heard a knock at the door, and when you opened the door both girls were standing there?"

"Yes, they were, Detective."

"And both girls said they were at Mickey Mouse Play House?"

"Yes, Detective."

"And there is no bodily harm done to either one of them?"

"Not even a missing hair."

"Mr. and Mrs. Long, did you see the car, or van that dropped them off?" the detective asked.

"No, Detective Mayfield, we didn't," Kevin replied.

"OK. Then that about wraps it up. If the girls remember anything, please give me a call."

"I will, and thank you, Detective, for all of your help."

"No problem, Kevin, take care."

Kevin watched as the three officers and the detective left.

Chapter Twenty-Eight

"Judge Mills, you have a phone call on line one."

"OK. Thank you, Mrs. Clark." Judge Mills picked up his phone as he sat behind his desk with his back to the open window.

"Judge Mills speaking."

"Hello, Judge Mills, how are you?"

"I'm fine, may I ask who I am speaking with?"

"Halo Rose."

"Halo, how is it going? What can I do for you?"

"Well, it came across my desk that you and Detective Hall have been having private meetings about Symone Rose. Now that everything is over with, I'm calling and asking you, are these rumors true?"

"Halo, Hall and I did in fact have two meetings, he was trying to get me to turn on Rose, but I wouldn't."

"So my next question is, why you never told us about these meetings?"

"Because there was so much going on at the time I didn't want to put more on the plate that was already full."

"The Rose family can respect that. We also respect your honesty and loyalty you have shown to the family. Ms. Rose would like to thank you in person for all you've done for her. Tonight she will have a car pick you up at eight p.m., how does that sound?"

"That sounds perfectly fine, Halo."

"I'll let her know. Take care, Judge Mills."

"You too, Halo." Judge Mills hung up the phone and thought back to both meetings he'd had with Detective Hall. He knew he was taking a chance going to meet up with Symone, but he was also afraid to tell Halo no. He took his hand and wiped his forehead off as he leaned back into his chair, thinking he was going to die tonight.

***

D.C. was laying in his bed sleeping when his phone went off. He rolled over and picked it up and saw that it was Masi calling him.

"Hello."

"Get dressed, it's time to ride out, I'll be there in ten minutes for you."

"Wait, where are we going?"

"Don't worry about that. Just be ready when I get there." Masi hung up the phone. D.C. jumped up and was outside when Masi pulled up.

"Yo, Masi, what's up?"

"Get in. We have to go put some work in."

"Where at?"

Masi cut his eyes at D.C.

"Don't worry about that, when we get there, we get there."

"Where's Muscle?"

"He's a few cars behind us making sure no one is following us. It's time for you to break the ice tonight, baby."

D.C. looked at Masi as he pressed *play* on the radio, blasting Jay-Z's *Black Album* as he smoked his blunt. It took them fifteen minutes to reach the docks. When they pulled up, there was a man outside the gate who nodded his head at Masi before letting him inside the dock yard.

"What is this place?"

"It's the docks, look, don't be asking a lot of questions, just be quiet and listen, that's all."

"D.C. saw Red Invee standing next to a man with a bag over his head tied to a pole. He watched her as she walked up to them.

"Hello, D.C., how are you?"

"I'm peace, how are you tonight?"

"Good, real good. So, I guess you are asking yourself what are you doing here, and who is that man tied to the pole with a bag over his head?"

"Yeah, that was a thought that crossed my mind."

"Don't worry. You will find out soon because you are going to take care of that business for me tonight. This will all be over soon."

***

A black limo pulled up in front of Judge Mills' house. It was eight p.m. on the head. Judge Mills opened his front door and stepped outside. He saw a man waiting for him at the limo. He took a deep breath as he walked to the limo.

"Hello, Mr. Mills, Ms. Rose is inside waiting for you."

Judge Mills watched as the man opened the limo door for him to step inside.

"Judge Mills, I'm glad you were able to see me tonight."

"Anything for you, Rose. So, can you tell me what this is all about?"

"Yes, it's about Detective Hall. He is digging up bones that have been buried for a very long time now and that's very bad for business for all of us, because when you start looking for things you might come across something you wish you hadn't."

"So how can I be a help to you in this matter?"

"I would like you to listen to something that I obtained from Detective Hall."

Judge Mills listened to the tape recording of him and Detective Hall's conversation:

"Judge Mills, I have you dead to the wrong, I have you on tape and video taking money from one of Symone Rose's thugs. Now I want to know why is she paying you off. Did you have your hands in Detective Boatman's murder?"

"No, Detective, I'm not a cop killer, but everyone gets paid under the table."

"So why are you getting paid under the table?"

"To make problems go away, that's why."

"Well, this time you're not going to make a problem go away. Symone Rose is going to be found guilty and you are going to make sure of it, if not then this video will be played on the news, do I make myself clear?"

Saynomore

"You don't know the kind of people you are dealing with, the friends they have, the people they know, the things they can have done to people like you."

"Just like D.A. Moore missing his head or Chief Tadem being kidnapped and killed in District Attorney Kendrick's shed, or A.D.A Kevin Long's girls being kidnapped. I know the kind of and I know what side of the law I stand on, Judge. Now like I said, Symone Rose will be found guilty." Judge Mills cut the tape recorder off and handed it back to Symone.

"Ms. Rose, I swear I wasn't going to find you guilty."

"I know, Judge, trust me, I do."

"So where are we going?"

"To see Detective Hall. He's waiting for us. I'm also told that we have an undercover officer waiting on us as well."

Judge Mills looked out the window as Symone reached into her bag and pulled out a *black and mild* and lit it; they were both quiet for the rest of the ride to the docks.

***

Iceman and Pistol walked up to Jamila as she was talking to Tasha.

"Mrs. LaCross, Symone texted me to let me know she will be here within the next twenty minutes, and Judge Mills is with her."

"Thank you, Iceman, for letting me know. Let's get ready to get our party started."

D.C. was watching everything. When he saw the lights from the limo pulling up at the dock gates, he looked at Masi.

"Yo, Masi, who is that?"

"Symone Rose. Let's get ready for the fuck shit."

Symone stepped out of the limo and walked over to Jamila and gave her a kiss on the cheek.

"So is that him?"

"Yeah, it is."

Judge Mills walked over to them.

"Good evening, Your Honor."

"Good evening to you, Mrs. LaCross."

"Judge Mills, you been a part of both our families, and you have helped us in more ways than one, but tonight is time you put blood on your hands."

Judge Mills looked at Jamila, lost, with no words to say.

Jamila nodded at Masi. Masi walked over to the man who was tied up on the pole and took the paper bag off his head. Judge Mills' eyes got as big as half dollar coins when he saw that it was Detective Hall.

"D.C., you good, homie?"

"Yeah, I'm good, Muscle. This shit is crazy, ain't that a cop on the pole?"

"Hell yeah, and you see that man over there talking with Red Invee and Rose?"

"Yeah, who is he?"

"Judge Mills."

"Why is he here?"

"Because one of them is going to die tonight and guess what?"

"I don't know, tell me."

"You are going to put the work in."

D.C. looked at Muscle.

"Welcome to the Mob."

"Come on, Judge Mills, let's all go talk to the man of the hour," Symone said.

Jamila waved Muscle and D.C. over.

"Detective Hall, lift your head up, someone wants to talk with you."

"It was very hard to find you, after going through your duffle bag, you had your I.D. in your jacket, but Iceman and Pistol are very loyal to me. All I have to do is ask and they get it done. That is why you are here now, and look who I brought down here to see you, the man you tried to bring down if he didn't find me guilty."

Detective Hall looked up at Judge Mills and spat on his shirt.

"Your day is coming, Mills, you think they give a fuck about you. They look at you just like they look at me, like a fucking cop. The only difference is you wear a fucking robe."

"No, Hall, the difference is I played on the team that won. That's why I'm standing here and looking at you over there."

Masi and Muscle walked up with D.C.

"D.C., come here!" Jamila said "I would like you to meet Detective Hall. Detective Hall, I would like you to meet undercover agent Corey Dorson."

Agent Corey looked at Jamila, but before he could say anything Muscle had his gun to the back of his head as Masi walked up to him and took his gun off his waist.

"Corey, you must not know who the fuck I am, but tonight you are going to learn. You wanted to be a part of my family, now you are playing with the big boys. It's going to be a kill or get killed night for you. You can kill Detective Hall with Judge Mills as a witness or I can have you killed tonight, then I'll have my two men here go out to the Bronx and have your sixty-five-year-old mother killed along with your two brothers. The choice is yours, so what's it going to be? Kill or be killed, Corey?"

"Corey, we are cops, we took an oath to bring down trash. If you kill me tonight you are no better than them."

"If I kill you tonight, my family lives, and that's all that matters to me."

Jamila handed Corey a loaded .45.

"Three shots to the head, Corey."

Corey looked around at everyone watching him as he took the gun from Jamila. He pointed it at Detective Hall's head; three shots were fired and Detective Hall's body went limp.

Masi took the gun from Corey and placed it in a plastic bag.

"Corey, now this is how it's going to go, from here on out you work for me. You're going to pull out from being undercover, and you are going to be my eyes and ears. You are going to let me know what I don't hear or see. The first time you don't let me know and I find out, it's not going to be good, just know that." Jamila looked at Symone. Symone nodded and handed Judge Mills a pocket knife.

"Judge Mills, walk over to Corey and cut a line down his right hand."

Judge Mills looked at Corey.

"Corey, this scar stands for disloyalty, dishonor, and untrustworthiness. Just know every time you look at your hand, Red Invee let you live and your life belongs to me now. Open your right hand. Now, Judge Mills, if you may."

Saynomore

Chapter Twenty-Nine

"Pistol, we are dealing with some real raw bitches, they be on point about everything."

"Iceman, Red Invee ain't no one to be fucked up with. She is too smart."

"What's the name of that shirt you're rocking, Pistol?"

"Oh, this that official 'gentlemen'. This is all I be really rocking."

"That shit is tough, homie."

"Yo, Iceman, look at baby girl walking up. Damn, she bad as fuck hands down."

Iceman and Pistol watched as the dark-skinned female walked their way. She had on a pair of skin-tight faded blue jeans, with rips in the front of them. She had on a black t-shirt that was hugging her flat stomach and her C-cup breasts. She had long locks that came down her back in a ponytail and she was wearing a pair of open-toed shoes, all black.

"Yo, Iceman, she looks just like Nia Long with locks."

"Yeah, Pistol, she is built tough."

As she walked up to them, she took her sunglasses off of her face.

"What's up, beautiful, how are you doing today?"

"I'm doing good."

"Well, let me introduce myself, my name is Iceman and this is my homie Pistol."

"Nice to meet you. My name is Victorious."

"That's a beautiful name. So you came to buy some jewelry today?"

"No, Iceman, I came to see Symone Rose. Is she here?"

Iceman and Pistol both looked at each other when she said that. "Yeah, she's here."

"Well, will you let her know I'm down here, Iceman?"

"Yeah, hold up, let me go get her, come inside."

Saynomore

When Iceman walked into Symone's office, she held up one finger to let him know to hold on one minute as she talked on the phone. Iceman closed the office door as Symone hung up the phone.

"Hey, Iceman, what's up?"

"There is a female downstairs who came here to see you."

"Does she have a name?"

"Yeah, she said her name is Victorious."

"What did she say her name was?"

"Victorious."

"No, it can't be. Take me to her." Symone grabbed her gun out her desk drawer and walked downstairs from her office to the main lobby. She stopped in her tracks when she saw Victorious standing there smiling at her.

"Oh my God, beautiful, come here, it's been so long."

Iceman and Pistol watched as Symone hugged Victorious.

"You look so beautiful, baby, and look at how long your hair is now. How old are you now?"

"Eighteen. I'll be nineteen in two more months." Symone smiled.

"Iceman, Pistol, this is my baby sister Victorious."

"Rose, this is your baby sister?"

"Yes, she is, Pistol. Iceman go get the car, we are going to see Red Invee. I know she going to be so happy to see you." Victorious just smiled.

***

"It's been two weeks and there still hasn't been any word on who murdered Vinnie, who had him killed? I want answers and I want them now. I want to know who he was talking to the day he was killed!"

"Fat Rob, I was told he was going to see Silvio Milano."

"Why was he going to New Jersey, Timmy?"

"I don't know, Fat Rob."

Fat Rob smoked his cigar, looking at the men in the room.

"Then you know what, gentlemen? I think it's time for us to pay Mr. Milano a visit. I would hate to start another war, but if Silvio's story doesn't add up or sound right, just know they drew first blood."

"When do you want to meet with them?"

"Let's set it up for this week, Timmy, because I want to do some digging in our own backyard first, then we will take it from there. Go get the car, I want to go see Red Invee."

***

Pistol opened up the limo door for Symone and Victorious to step out, as Iceman watched the scene as they walked into *Jelani's*.

"Have you ever been in here before, Victorious?"

"No, never, but this place is fly as hell, sis."

"I said those same words the first time I stepped in here."

Iceman and Pistol stayed at the front door with Masi and Muscle.

"Come on, her office is this way."

Once off the elevator, Symone opened Jamila's office door. Jamila was looking at all her birds when they walked into her office.

"Jamila, guess who came to see us today. Beautiful!"

"Victorious, is that you?"

"Yes, it is," Victorious answered.

Smiling, Jamila walked up to her and gave her a big hug.

"Oh my God, come sit down, tell me how you been."

"I been good, real good."

"How's mom?"

"She's good."

"Does she know you are here with us, Victorious?"

"Yes, I told her I was coming to see both of you."

Jamila looked at Symone and smiled.

"What did she say?"

"That she told Symone that this day was coming."

Symone and Jamila both laughed.

"So, do you have a car, Victorious?"

"No, Jamila."

"So, we will have to do something about that, but look at you, you are so beautiful, baby girl." Jamila's phone started going off. "Hold on one minute, Victorious. I have to get that."

Victorious watched as Jamila walked to her desk. Symone watched Jamila's facial expression as she hung up the phone.

"Victorious, go sit at the second seat on the right from the head of the table, don't talk, just sit quietly, baby girl." Symone walked up to Jamila

"What's going on?"

"Tasha just told me that Fat Rob is here with four of his men and they need to talk to me."

When the door opened, Symone looked at Iceman and Pistol and gestured for them to go stand next to Victorious as Muscle and Masi stayed next to Jamila and Symone.

"Fat Rob, please come in, how can I help you?"

Fat Rob walked up to Symone and gave her a kiss on both cheeks, then he walked up to Jamila and gave her a kiss on the hand then a kiss on the cheek.

"Jamila, thank you for seeing me."

"Please take a seat, can I get you water, wine, or something stronger?"

"Something stronger, Mrs. LaCross."

Jamila nodded to Masi.

"So here's the thing, someone killed Vinnie two weeks ago as he was headed to New Jersey to see Silvio, but his limo was cut off and shot up. It was a set-up from the very beginning. Now, I'm just trying to put two and two together and I was hoping you could help me out, to get to the bottom of this."

"To be honest, I really don't know much, except for what I saw and heard on the news."

At that time Masi came back with two glasses and a bottle of Grey Goose.

"But, I will try and see what I can find out for you, Fat Rob, but I'm not making you any promises."

"I thank you for just trying. So, how does it feel to have the load off of your shoulders as the head Don?"

With a light laugh Jamila said:

"Relaxing. I just hope everyone respects everyone else's turf."

"As I do, Red Invee." Fat Rob got up and kissed Jamila's cheek; with both his hands he held her arms.

"Thank you for all you can do for me, Red Invee."

"You're welcome."

Jamila watched as Fat Rob and his men left. Jamila looked at Symone.

"Do you have any idea who hit Vinnie up?"

"No, I don't."

"You know what? That's none of our business. We have our little sister here with us now." When Jamila said that, Muscle and Masi looked at Victorious.

"Victorious, come here, beautiful."

"Yes, Jamila."

"Muscle, Masi, meet my baby sister Victorious. Victorious, these are my two hittas. Victorious, did you eat yet?"

"No."

"Good, Masi, order us everything on today's special. Order enough food for the eight of us and two bottles of Ace of Spades."

***

Agent Brooks walked into the briefing room where Special Agent Carter was waiting on him with Special Agent Corey.

"Sorry I'm late, now what happened out there, Special Agent Corey?"

"I was made by Red Invee. She knew who I was all along."

"What happened to your hand?"

"When she told me who I was, the first chance I had I took off running, I hopped a wire fence and cut my hand. When I looked back no one was chasing me, they just let me run off."

"What can you tell us about Red Invee's operation?"

"Nothing, they kept me in the blind the whole time."

"So what did you do for the eight weeks you were undercover?"

Special Agent Brooks sat quietly and just listened to everything Agent Corey said as Agent Carter questioned him.

"Parties, clubs, females. Masi did say after I put some work in, they will start dealing with me on the work withwhatever I needed."

"Who all was there the night she pulled your cover?"

"Jamila, Masi, Muscle, Symone, Iceman, and Pistol. I don't know the guys she had as bodyguards she had walking around, sir."

"Do you think they made Agent Melissa?"

"I don't know, sir."

"Agent Brooks."

"Yes, sir."

"Pull Agent Melissa in, let's get on update with her ASAP and we need to know how Corey's ID was blown. We might have a mole. We need to start checking phone records, emails, we need to dig this mole out now."

"Yes, sir."

"Corey, you will be placed somewhere for the next few months until things cool down for you."

"Understood, sir."

"Good, I'll catch up to you in a few."

Agent Brooks watched as Agent Corey walked out of the briefing room.

"What do you think, sir?"

"He's lying about how he got that cut on his right hand. That cut stands for dishonor, disloyalty, and untrustworthiness. I know a few ex-mafia members who have that same cut. If they made him, they made his family."

"So why do you think they let him go, sir?"

"There are enough killings of cops in the city, they don't want the heat on them right now."

"That's a good point, sir."

"Brooks, pull Agent Melissa back, get on track about finding this mole and keep me updated on everything."

"Will do, sir."

Special Agent Carter picked up his briefcase and walked out of the briefing room.

Saynomore

"Please do sit—"

Special Agent Carter picked up his briefcase and walked out of the waiting room.

Chapter Thirty

"Ladies, ladies, what do we have so far?" Perk G asked as he looked around the table full of drugs.

"We have twenty-six kilos already sealed up with the stamp on it," Alana said.

"Good, real good, how long before the rest of it is done?"

"I can't tell you that. This was a big shipment this time. We still have so much at the other location, Perk G. If I would have to guess it's six of us working maybe two more days at the most."

"I can work with that, Alana." Perk G walked off, pulled out his phone and called Halo.

"What's good, homie?"

"Slow motion right now, tell me something good, Perk G."

"I have twenty-six ready for you to pick up."

"Say less, I'll be there in about two hours. Let me call Iceman, Pistol, and Slim Boogie and let them know to be ready for me."

"Cool, I'll see you in a few hours." Perk G hung up the phone and walked to the corner and rolled up a blunt and watched the females in their G-strings and topless state as they worked on the tables bagging up the Red Flame as he smoked his blunt.

***

District Attorney Kendrick sat at his desk as he worked on his computer, going over his caseload, when there was a knock at his office door.

"Come in." D.A. Kendrick stopped what he was doing and watched as his office door opened up.

"Good morning, Katrina."

"Good morning, Kendrick. How are you feeling this morning?"

With a deep breath Kendrick looked at Katrina.

"I'm making it."

"That's all we can do as prosecutors. I overheard that Kevin's girls are at home and safe."

"Yeah, two days now."

"Have you talked to him since?"

"No, not yet. I don't think he wants to talk with me. I should have never dragged him into this. Because of me his children were kidnapped, Symone walked. Everything was over nothing. Cindy might still be in danger. This whole case was a bust."

"It wasn't a total loss. What did you learn from all of this?"

"How to lose a friend, but I guess I wanted Symone so bad I didn't realize I was putting everyone in harm's way."

"You can't win all of them, Kendrick, but if I were you I'd pick up the phone and call Kevin if anything else."

"I guess you are right."

Katrina turned around and went to walk out the door. As she opened it, Kevin was walking in.

"Hey, Kevin."

"Hey, Katrina."

Kendrick walked around his desk to meet Kevin.

"I'll let you two talk," Katrina said as she closed the office door."

"Kevin, let me say I'm sorry for pulling you in this bullshit with me."

"You know what, Kendrick? Now that my girls are home and I've had some time to think and clear my head, you did not know any of this was going to happen, nobody did. I did hear about what you did to get my girls back. Thanks, man." Kevin walked up to Kendrick and gave him a hug. He smiled at him, and with nothing else to be said Kevin walked out of the office, closing the door behind him.

Chapter Thirty-One

Agent Brooks sat on the hood of his car, smoking a Kool under the bridge as he waited for Agent Melissa to pull up. He looked around at the garbage on the ground and the people sleeping in cardboard boxes; that's when he saw the headlights coming his way from Melissa's car. When the car stopped, Melissa stepped out and walked up to Agent Brooks.

"Hello, sir."

"How are you doing, agent?"

"I'm fine, sir."

"And how is it going with the Rose family?"

"It's coming along, sir. I've been hanging out with one of Symone's top men. His name is Pistol. He hasn't really opened up to me too much, but he is starting to."

"Well, I called you out here tonight because Agent Corey's cover has been blown."

"They made him. How did they make him?"

"We think there is a mole at the station who gave him up. Carter wants me to pull you for now."

"Sir, not right now, you can't."

"Agent, it's above my head. As of right now you are off the case until further notice, agent, we are going to have you relocated to somewhere until things cool down."

"Sir, this isn't right. I've been busting my ass on this case."

"I know, agent, but your well-being is more important to me than Symone Rose being behind bars. Go home, pack your bags and be ready to make the move within the next twenty-four hours."

"Sir."

"There's nothing more to say, agent." Agent Brooks got in his car and drove off leaving Agent Melissa standing there.

***

"Victorious, come have a seat over here on the deck with me and Symone, I have to ask you something."

Saynomore

"What's up, sis?"
Jamila looked at Symone. Symone nodded at Jamila.
"What happened in Long Island?"
Victorious looked at both of her sisters.
"How did you find out what happened?"
"Mom sent me an email and when I called her, she told me everything she knew, so now I'm asking you to tell me your part of the story?"
"I was talking to this guy for a few weeks. His ex-girlfriend came by his house and tried to jump on me, but he wouldn't let her. A few weeks passed. I was leaving from a friend of mine's house walking. She saw me on Smith Street behind the school on my way to his house. She waited until I was in the path. She ran up on me with a gun and tried to hit me with it, I ducked down, we started fighting over the gun, I fell and she shot me in the back, but it grazed me. B-more came running in the woods where the path was. He grabbed her, and she dropped the gun. I picked it up and shot her dead in the head, killing her. B-more looked at me and before he could say anything I killed him. I looked around, nobody was around, I took his phone and ran home. I told mom everything and she told me she told Symone this day was coming."
"Where the gun and phone at? Symone asked.
Victorious looked at Symone and passed Symone her purse.
"Victorious, did you tell anyone you were going to B-more's house?"
"No, not a soul."
"Good," Both Symone and Jamila said.
"I already know what you are thinking, Jamila, I'm going to get rid of the gun and phone."
"Good and I'll see what I can find out. Until then, Victorious, you can stay with me. Victorious, why did you kill B-more?" Jamila asked.
"Because the look on his face said he was going to call the police."
"You did right then, beautiful. Come on, let me get you set up in one of my Brownstones."

Chapter Thirty-Two

Symone sat at the bar while she was drinking a blue margarita when Katrina walked in.

"Hey, Ms. Rose."

Symone looked at Katrina and put her glass down.

"Hey, beautiful, I'm glad you could make it. So, Jamila told me what you did for me. So, I'm here to make you an offer. Do you want to be a part of my family?"

"It would be an honor."

"Nobody comes into the family without getting their hands dirty."

"It's a sign of loyalty."

Katrina looked at Symone. "What do I have to do?" Symone picked up her glass and took a sip then looked at Katrina. "Kill Kendrick."

The look on Symone's face and the expression she had let Katrina know she wasn't playing.

"When does it have to be done?"

"I'm giving you one week. Do you think you can pull it off within that time?" asked Symone.

"I'll do what I have to do."

"There's one more thing I need to tell you, Katrina."

"And what's that?'

"If you don't pull it off within a week, then you die."

"Where do you want his body at?" asked Katrina.

"Make it disappear, no body—no case. Do you have a gun?"

"Yea, I have one."

"Good, but take this one, it's clean, nothing will come back to you. Make sure you have an alibi for where you was at the time of the murder. Pass me your bag."

Symone placed the black .9mm into Katrina's bag.

"You have my number, call me when it's done."

Symone got up and walked out the bar at *Destiny's*.

***

Saynomore

Muscle opened up the limo door at Gino's house for Jamila to step out.

"Gino, thank you for seeing me," said Jamila as she walked up to him and gave him a kiss on both cheeks.

"So what brings you up here and out of the city?" asked Gino.

"Is there some place we can talk?"

"Sure, let's go sit in the back on the deck. It's cool back there next to the trees under the shade," replied Gino.

Jamila was quiet the whole time, not saying a word until they reached the backyard.

"What's going on, Jamila?" asked Gino.

"Fat Rob came to see me yesterday asking me do I know anything about Vinnie's murder. I told him the truth, which was no, then he asked me if I could look into it, but the one question I've been asking myself is, who would want Vinnie dead?"

"Red Invee, Vinnie wasn't right at all. He was doing a lot of dirt under the table that no one knew about."

"Like what?" asked Jamila.

"Come walk with me, let me show you something."

Gino showed Jamila the spot that his car blew up at.

"What happened?"

About three weeks ago I was on my way to Brooklyn and it rained that night. The next morning when me and Joey was getting ready to leave, I saw footprints in the grass. Then the hood of the car had water running down the sides as if the hood was raised up. I told Joey the door handle was dry. He looked at me funny then I saw he was still a little way in the yard from where I was. I walked back to him and took the car keys and pressed the alarm on the keychain and the car blew up. Right then I knew Joey set me up but I had no proof so I got a hold to his phone. I sent a few texts out and just like I thought, I got a text back that said, *Good, come to the club.*

"It was Vinnie, wasn't it, Gino?" asked Red Invee.

"Yea, it was, so I took care of Vinnie first with the help of a few friends then I took care of Joey myself and left him to the wild animals to eat in the woods."

"So you killed Vinnie?" asked Red Invee.

"I had all the right to," replied Gino.

"So what about Fat Rob asking questions?"

"I've known Fat Rob very well. He just wants to make it look good, that's all, but if it comes down to it he can go swimming with the fishes too. I ain't make it this far into the game by being messy."

"I understand. I also need your help, Gino, my baby sister killed two people in Long Island and I need to know what they know down there."

"I have a few friends I can reach out to down there that should know something. Where did it happen at?" asked Gino

"Deer Park."

"I'll look into it this evening."

"Thank you, Gino!"

Gino walked Jamila back to her limo and watched as it pulled away before walking back into his house.

***

"Cindy, someone's here to see you," one officer said to her that was watching her in witness protection.

"Who was it?" asked Cindy.

"D.A. Kendrick."

Cindy got up and walked to the living room where Kendrick was waiting on her at.

"Cindy, how are you holding up?"

"I hate it here. When can I leave?"

"That's what I came to talk to you about. Now that the trial is over there are a few locations we can set you up at," said Kendrick.

"I'm listening."

"How does LA sound to you? Or GA? Wherever you decide to go there will be a job waiting on you, a house and thirty thousand dollars ready to be wired to your bank account."

"What about Symone Rose? Is she going to come looking for me?" asked Cindy.

"Don't worry about her," said Kendrick, "you are going to have a new identity and whatever location you choose is going to be confident. So you shouldn't have any worries."

"Okay then. I want to move to LA then, to the West Coast."

"That's good, be ready to leave within the next seventy-two hours—and thank you, Cindy, it took a lot of guts to do what you did. I'll see you in a few days and next time you see me this whole thing will be over."

"Good, then I can't wait to see you next time, Kendrick."

Chapter Thirty-Three

Tasha walked in her front door to see Mike, her baby father, sitting at the kitchen table talking with her sis.
"Hello, Tasha."
"Mike, what are you doing here?"
"I came to see my son and talk with you."
"Sis, I'll let you two talk and I'll take lil' man out to eat then to the park for a little while."
"OK. Mike, why are you really here?" asked Tasha.
"I came for our son, that's why I'm here, Tasha. I heard that you quit your job and now I see you in the paper next to Jamila LaCross."
"Mike, my son is not going nowhere, and *yes* I'm in the paper next to Mrs. LaCross. I work for her. I'm with her every day. I'm the manager at her restaurant and I have been working for her the past few years."
"Tasha, I don't want my son mixed up in that MOB lifestyle," replied Mike.
"Mike, there is no such thing as the mob, look how you sound. Mike, I think it's time for you to go."
"Tasha, you heard what I said. I'm here for my son."
"And you heard what I said, my son is not going anywhere."
As Tasha went to walk past Mike, he grabbed her arm and pushed her to the wall.
"No, you heard what I said, Tasha!" When Mike turned his head and looked down, Tasha had her 9mm pressed up against his stomach.
"Nigga, if you don't let me go, you are going to fuck up and die. Now I don't know who the fuck you think I am, but fuck around and have 12 men searching for your body!" said Tasha angrily.
Mike took two steps back and looked at Tasha.
"I don't know who the fuck you are no more."
Tasha smacked him in the face with the gun, dropping him to the floor. She stood over him and pointed her gun at Mike's face as he looked up at her.

"A bad bitch, nigga, the only reason you ain't dead is because of our son. Get the fuck up off my floor and get the fuck out of my house before I have to tell our son a sad story about his father's death."

Tasha watched as Mike got up off the floor. As he was walking out the door, Tasha called him. Mike turned around and looked at Tasha.

"Respect the code of silence."

Mike closed the door and walked off to his car.

***

"Jamila, sis, your house needs to be on MTV cribs, this shit is fly."

"Thanks, Victorious, it came with a lot of blood, sweat, and tears. It wasn't easy getting here. I remember praying to God asking him to please remove my enemies from my life and one by one my friends started dropping from my life. Victorious, I know you see the life me and Symone live. It looks good from the outside, but it's not all fun and games and I don't want you getting caught up in this lifestyle because once you get caught up there is no way out but death. Look, baby girl, have a seat on the love seat and I'll go get us something to drink and eat. I'll be right back."

Victorious looked around the house from where she was sitting. She wanted everything her older sister had and more. When Jamila came back to the living room, she had in her hands two cold sodas and a bag of chips.

"Okay, let's talk, cutie. I have a friend of mine who is going to make your problem disappear."

"Thank you so much, sis!" replied Victorious excitedly.

"You are welcome. You know me and Symone's father got killed living this life in the worst way by his own friend. And the man who I loved tried to kill me. This is a kill-or-be-killed life. The mob is just not about killing, it's also about thinking. It's like playing chess; the point is to always win. Sometimes you have to give up a power piece to win."

"Jamila, I been reading all the news stories about you and Symone. I even saw when you was arrested. Me and mom watched it one the news together. She knew one day I would be here sitting next to you."

"So I'm assuming that your mind is made up already about living this life?"

Victorious just nodded at Jamila.

"Then you are going to do it the right way then, do I make myself clear?"

"Yes."

"I'll be right back." Jamila walked off and went to her study. She came back a few minutes later with her father's two books, *The 48 Laws of Power* and *The Art of War*."

My father had me read these two books for years, now I want you to read them and I'll get you a job in the criminal field. You are going to be my ghost until you get everything down pack, you understand?" asked Jamila.

"Yes, I do," replied Victorious.

"Good. Before you are twenty-one you will have your own house like this, I promise. Now if you go upstairs to the right, that first room is yours for now and I will call Ma and let her know you are staying."

"Thank you, sis!"

"Victorious, I got you, baby girl, from here on out."

Saynomore

Chapter Thirty-Four

Cindy looked out the window as she was being taken to LA for her new life, leaving everything she had behind. DA Kendrick did everything he told her he would do. He promised her a new life, and he delivered on his promise.

"How long before we reach LA?" asked Cindy.

"It's going to be a while Ms. Morris."

Cindy leaned back in the car seat and put her head set on and played Mary J. Blige's "Everything" as she closed her eyes, and was vibing to the music. She hated being around police officers all day because she couldn't do what she wanted to do. She wanted to get high so bad, but she couldn't around them and it was driving her crazy to the point she felt she was going to break. In her mind she knew taking the stand against Symone Rose could cost her her life, and if she was going to die, she was going to die high.

***

DA Kendrick walked out of his office to the break room where he saw Katrina sitting down drinking a cup of coffee and reading the newspaper. He always liked her from her long black and gold locks to her beautiful smile. Her honey brown skin tone and her hourglass body. He had a smile on his face as he walked up to her.

"What are you reading about this morning?"

"I'm just looking over the stock market; it's how I start my day," said Katrina.

"Why are you here so early?" asked Katrina.

"I had to sign all the paperwork on Cindy Morris this morning."

"I know you are glad you have that load off your shoulders."

"Yea, I am."

"So where did she decide to relocate to?" asked Katrina

"LA, she has a job waiting for her, a house set up for her. She has a whole new life."

"That's good. You took care of her, Kendrick. So what's next on your caseload?"

"I don't know yet, but how would you like to go to dinner with me?"

Katrina looked at Kendrick then smiled. "When would you like to go out?"

"How does tomorrow night sound?"

"That sounds good, Kendrick, so what time will you be picking me up?"

"How does eight p.m. sound to you?"

"Good to me, Kendrick."

Kendrick got up from the table and said, "I'll see you then."

"I can't wait, Kendrick."

Katrina watched as Kendrick walked off.

***

Fat Rob smiled as he shook Silvio Milano's hand.

"You have a beautiful place here."

"Thank you, Fat Rob. Let me introduce you to my guys— Lil Jon, Snake and Freeman."

"Nice to meet you guys. I believe you know my guys already."

"Yea, I do, so tell me, what brings you by?"

"To my understanding, Silvio, Vinnie was on his way to see you when he was set up and killed," said Fat Rob.

"I heard about that and I'm sorry to hear about what happened to Vinnie, but Vinnie had no cause to come see me. I haven't spoken to Vinnie in a very long time, it's been over a year."

"All that tells me, Silvio, is that there is foul play somewhere down the line."

"Fat Rob, where did you get this information from?"

"Someone from my family told me that was the last thing that Bull told him. Silvio, thank you for seeing me today."

"Anytime," Silvio said as he shook Fat Rob's hand.

Chapter Thirty-Five

Symone sat behind her desk as she was going over all the shipments this week on the docks when Slim Boogie knocked on her office door. She took her attention off of her computer as her office door opened up.

"Ms. Rose, Mr. Gino Sabrano is here to see you."

"Thank you, Slim, bring him up here for me."

"Mr. Sabrano, please come in and have a seat. Slim Boogie, you can leave us."

Slim nodded as he walked out the door, closing it behind him.

"Mr. Sabrano, can I offer you something to drink?" asked Symone.

"Yes, please, do you have brandy?"

"Yes, I do, with ice or without ice?"

"Without. I stopped by to bring you something, Symone."

"And what is that, Mr. Sabrano?" asked Symone as she walked back to the table with two glasses of brandy. Gino handed Symone a paper bag with $100,000 inside.

"Thank you for your help with Vinnie. I knew I could count on you to get the job done."

"You're welcome. I do have one question to ask you."

"And what is that?"

"Who was the man in the Hummer?" asked Symone, curiously

"He was one of my guys. I had him there to make it look good on both of our ends. He told me how your men jumped out the van with AR-15's and lite the limo up," said Sabrano.

"My promise to you was that my shooters don't miss and I don't break my promise."

"Ms. Rose, I really do have a great deal of respect for you."

"Mr. Sabrano, so anytime that you call the Rose family we will be there. I don't know if you know this, but Fat Rob did come by *Jelani's* the other day asking questions about Vinnie."

"What type of questions?"

"He asked Jamila did she know anything about who set him up. She told him no, but the look in his eyes said a different story like something ain't right."

"Symone, how do you kill two birds with one stone?" asked Sabrano

"I don't know, tell me."

"Just make sure they are both at the same spot when you throw the stone."

"Are you trying to tell me something, Mr. Sabrano?"

"Symone, some statements don't need to be followed up by a question and we don't need our secret to get out if he keeps asking questions, and we don't need that."

"So when you say kill two birds with one stone you really mean the whole Lenacci family?" asked Symone.

Gino got up and walked to the door before turning around and looking back at Symone.

"There's nothing else to be said, Rose, have a nice day."

Gino opened the door and walked out of it.

***

Kendrick pulled up at Katrina's house at 8 p.m. in his blue F-150 Ford pick-up truck. He stepped out with a box of candy and flowers as he walked towards the front door. He knocked two times before the door opened.

"Hello, handsome, you look nice, are those for me?"

"Yes, they are beautiful, and you look outstanding tonight."

"Thank you," replied Katrina.

Kendrick was looking at how the dress Katrina had on was hugging her body, showing off her shape and how the three- inch heels were making her calf muscles stand out. She was wearing a set of diamond earrings. Her hair was coming down over her face with curls at the tip. He loved her smile, and the red lipstick made everything perfect.

"So where are you taking me tonight, sir?" asked Katrina.

"To a little jazz spot off 31st. It's a nice little spot I go to every now and then to eat. I think you are going to like it."

Kendrick walked Katrina to his truck and opened the door for her to step in.

"This is a very nice truck you have here," said Katrina.

"Thank you, I just got it about two years ago," replied Kendrick.

"I didn't know you was into jazz, Kendrick."

"You know, it's a long story, but after the Wall Street shooting case, I was hungry. I didn't want to wait in line at any other food spot so I saw a sign on the window that said *hot meals*. So I walked in and been going there ever since. Katrina, why are you single?"

"I guess a woman of power like me makes men feel like I'm too strong willed for them or they just are weak minded," replied Katrina.

"Come on, let me just find a parking space for us."

***

Pistol looked out his office window at everyone on the floor. Men paying for lap dances, the females dancing on the poles to the people at the bar buying drinks. It's been three weeks and he hadn't seen Kia nor had she answered his phone calls. He walked away from the window back to his desk when he saw Ro, one of his girls walking up the stairs to his office with two bags in her hands as he was lighting his blunt. She opened the door.

"What you got for me, Ro?" asked Pistol.

"This is the money the girls bring in this week from the floor and in this bag is the money from the Red Flame. Two hundred and eighty-five thousand dollars, and we still have two kilos left."

"Okay, let's try and push that on the floor this week. Now how much money did the ladies bring in?" asked Pistol.

"Seventy-five thousand dollars," replied Ro.

"Business is doing good for us. You know what? Start pushing the Red Flame today and I'm raising the price to all the private booths from two hundred dollars to three hundred dollars. Let the girls know that, Ro."

Saynomore

"I'll do that now."

Pistol watched as Ro left his office. He picked up the phone and called Perk G; after two rings, Perk G picked up.

"Yo, what's good, Pistol?" asked Perk G.

"I need you to pull up on me around five o'clock, but right now I'm about to head down 285."

"Okay, cool, Pistol, but I ain't going to be able to see you until tomorrow, but I got you."

"Say less, Bro, now let me call Rose and I'll hit you back, fam."

"Copy that."

Pistol hung up the phone, put his blunt out and picked up the two bags of money and walked off to the safe.

***

"Kendrick, this place is nice, very nice."

I had a feeling you would like it. Wait till you taste the food; it's to die for."

"You know out of all the years I lived in Brooklyn I never knew this place was here," said Katrina.

"That's because you are so wrapped up in your career, you don't take time for yourself," replied Kendrick.

"I do take time out for me; matter of fact, when we leave here, I want to take you somewhere."

"And where is that?" asked Kendrick, curious.

"A place where I go when I want to block the world out."

Kendrick looked at Katrina and smiled as the waiter walked over to take their orders. "Hello, are you ready to make your order?"

"Yes, we are. I will take the house steak with mac cheese and a coke with no ice."

"And for you, Ms.?"

"I think I will have the same thing, but I want ice with my drink," replied Katrina

"Okay, your orders will be out within the next twenty minutes."

After eating and dancing to the slow jazz music, they talked for a few more minutes before heading out to Katrina's place of peace.

"Katrina, you come here?" asked Kendrick.

"All the time and just look at the water. You will never see anybody out here."

Kendrick just looked at the moonlight over the black lake and the many woods that surrounded the lake. It was peaceful there.

"How did you find this place?" asked Kendrick. "There's not a house around for miles."

"I found it a while back when I was hiking in these woods."

When Kendrick turned around to face Katrina she was a few feet back pointing a black .380 at him.

"This is why you bring me out here to kill me?" asked Kendrick. "This is what this whole night was about?"

"I didn't want it to end like this for you, but you left me no choice."

"There is always a choice, Katrina."

"Not in this case, there's not."

"So what will the headlines read in the newspaper, Katrina? Dead DA body found floating in the lake?"

"No, Kendrick, your body will never be found."

Kendrick went to jump at Katrina; that's when she let off three shots to the chest, killing him. His body hit the ground. Katrina stripped off all of his clothes and tied chains with bricks onto him and pushed his body into the lake. She watched as it disappeared to the bottom. She picked up the three shell casings from the gun and turned around and left. She then drove Kendrick's truck a few miles out upstate NY and wiped it down and left it in the woods out of sight.

Saynomore

Chapter Thirty-Six

Victorious looked around Crystal's office. Crystal took Victorious on as an intern, as a favor for Jamila. It was Victorious' first day, and all eyes was on the new female. The men couldn't take their eyes off her.

"Victorious, let me show you around," said Crystal.

"Over here to the left is where we take all the phone calls."

Victorious waved to the three females and one guy that was sitting down answering phone calls.

"Now over here is where we post the 'most wanted' list up at. Here is where the most wanted men and females are at. But not just thugs. I'm talking big time players, drug lords, contract killers. Now in this room is where we have our ongoing investigations and closed cases, but people we still keep an eye out on just in case we need to put a search warrant out for them."

Victorious walked up to the billboard with all the pictures on them. And was looking at the pictures of her older sisters on the board. Crystal walked up to the board.

"Jamila LaCross and Symone Rose, two of NYC's deadliest and dangerous, notorious females who come out of NYC boroughs who took NYC by storm, leaving bodies everywhere they go."

"Are they under investigation?" asked Victorious. "That's why their pictures are still up there?"

"No, they are not. We can never get them on nothing. Undercover officers come up missing or just want to get off the case. Queens and Brooklyn's curse and blessings. Come on, let me show you where CSI is at."

"Crystal, before we leave, who are these two people under their photos?"

"They are two of the undercover officers who we pulled out because Officer Corey was made."

Victorious looked at the pictures one more time before following Crystal to the CSI department.

"Now that I showed you around, let me show you what you will be doing. How are you on a computer?" asked Crystal.

"Good. I can type up to sixty words a minute."

"Good because you will be logging in all open reports and the ones we closed. Let me show you how, come on."

***

Katrina handed Symone the 9mm in a brown paper bag.

"Was it hard for you to do?" asked Symone.

"No, it wasn't."

"That's good to hear," said Symone as she drank her morning cup of coffee.

"Come have a seat next to me. Now what you need to know is that Mob's number one rule. Respect the Code of Silence no matter what."

Katrina nodded at Symone. As she talked, Symone reached into her top right desk drawer and handed Katrina a stack of money.

"The next thing is, nothing is for free. Here is twenty thousand dollars for the job you handled."

Symone handed her the money. "Here are my rules, not the Mafia rules, *mine*. #1 - Never talk to no one about our family business. #2 - Never talk to no one about what me and you talk about. #3 - Always show your loyalty to the family. #4 - Never question me. #5 - Always keep two guns on you at all times. And #6 - Never trust no one. Right now, I need you now here, you are to protect the family but you will get paid just like everyone else. You are now a made woman, Katrina Rose. I have one more gift for you." Symone handed Katrina a VVS yellow diamond ring. "Wear it with pride."

"Symone, are we a part of the LaCross family?" asked Katrina.

"No, we are not. We are our own family and Jamila has her own family. Come take a ride with me, we have a meeting to go to, plus you need to meet your new family members."

***

Fat Rob smoked his cigar as he looked around at everyone in the room.

"Someone is not playing right," said Fat Rob.

"Do you think it's someone in the seven families?"

"I don't know, Lil John. I done spoke with Red Invee and Rose, as well as Silvio Milano. Someone is not talking that knows something. And when I find out who it is I'll have hot bullets for they ass and whoever is with them."

"Do you want to go have a talk with Gino?"

"You know what? Fuck Gino. For all I know he had his hands in Vinnie's murder. He ain't come see me yet to talk about what happened to Vinnie or show his respect to the family. All he wants to do is sit in his house on the hill."

Fat Rob got up and walked past everyone to the window.

"You know what? Now that I think about it, I do remember seeing Gino's driver here two maybe three weeks ago. What's his name?"

"Joey."

"Yea, that's it, Lil John. Get in touch with him. I want to know what him and Vinnie was talking about before Vinnie was killed," said Fat Rob.

"I'll get on that right away, Fat Rob."

"Thanks, Lil John. As for everyone else here, if I think or find out that Gino had something to do with Vinnie's death, he fucking dies and that's me pushing the fucking button."

***

Katrina had a black hoodie on as she walked into the casino with Symone. She had her head down so no one could see her face.

"Hello, Ms. Rose, how are you today?"

"I'm doing good. Is everyone ready?"

"Yes, everyone is upstairs in the office waiting on you."

"Good," said Symone. "Come, let's not keep them waiting on us." Iceman walked Symone and Katrina to the office. When the door opened up, everyone looked at Symone walking into the office. They all stood up from their seats out of respect for her. Katrina took off her hoodie once in the office.

Saynomore

"Everyone, I would like you to meet Katrina; she is a part of the family now," said Symone as Katrina took a seat at the table.

"I called you all here today because Fat Rob is asking too many questions about Vinnie's murder."

"May I speak, Ms. Rose?"

"The table is yours, Halo."

Halo looked at everyone. "Vinnie's murder has nothing to do with us, so why do we care if he is asking questions?"

"Because we do have something to do with his death."

Everyone looked at Symone.

"I was the one who had him killed as a favor to someone. Now the same person is asking me to take out the whole family."

"Ms. Rose, with the utmost respect we will never question your loyalty. You made this family and you never turned your back on us, but I feel we should at least know who we are putting work in for."

"You are right, Slim Boogie, you do have the right to know. If I choose to tell you and I don't, so when I say it's time just be ready. Because we are going to kill the whole family. Now for you at this table who don't know, Katrina took care of the DA Kendrick who tried to put me in prison for life. And because of her we was able to kidnap ADA Kevin's two little girls, and that alone got my case dismissed. Thank you, Iceman and Pistol, for taking care of that business for me. And thank you, Katrina, for taking care of your end for me. Perk G, how is the Red Flame moving?"

"Good, we are down to our last hundred kilos."

"And how much did we take in?" asked Symone.

"Six million dollars and the money is already at the second location in the safe."

"Good then there is nothing else to be talked about, and before we leave—how is everything at the strip club, Pistol?"

"Everything is a hundred percent, Rose."

"Okay, then," Rose stood up. "Katrina, come on, we have other business to go over. Perk G, I will put a new order in this week for a new shipment, so be ready for it."

"I will, Rose."

Mob Ties 6

Everyone watched as Symone and Katrina left the office.

Saynomore

Chapter Thirty-Seven

"Fat Rob, I've been to see the Gambino family, Scott family and a few joints I know Joey be at."

"And what did you come up with, Lil John?"

"Nobody's seen him in the last three weeks."

"That's because he's swimming with the fishes. Gino is covering his tracks. Send the boys at him. I want everything around him killed; if it breathes it dies," said Fat Rob as he looked at the lake in his backyard.

"Lil John."

"Yea, boss?"

"Everything dies tonight."

Lil John turned around and walked off leaving Fat Rob at the lake. Fat Rob watched the sunset over the lake. He turned around and walked to his limo. His driver opened the door for him to get in. Inside he looked at his watch and saw it was 7:45 p.m. He pulled out his cigar and lit it as his driver drove him to the house.

***

Gino sat in his living room with lines of coke on the table, watching the dog race, cursing at the TV because his dog was losing the race he betted on. He heard the dogs barking and looked at his monitor, and saw men running up to his house in all black with guns in their hands.

"What the fuck!" He ran and cut all the lights off. That's when he heard the back door getting kicked in. He pulled his gun out and ran to the living room wall. He looked in the mirror on the wall and saw two men with guns in their hands walking down the hallway. He kneeled down and as they were walking through the door, he jumped up and shot them—one in the face and the other in the neck. He took off running to the left hallway. That's when he was shot in the right shoulder by one of the guys from outside the house through the window. Gino hit the floor and dropped his gun. "Fuck." He got up holding his shoulder. "Ya want to kill me, then come the fuck on. I'll kill all you sons of bitches. Do you know who the fuck I am! I'm Gino fucking Sabrano."

Gino grabbed two guns from out of his bookshelves and put his back against the wall. Gino had blood running down his back. His arm was hurting from the shot to his back shoulder. He was looking at the front door. He took a deep breath and aimed both guns at the front door. He watched as the front door was kicked down. He let out a loud scream and started shooting at the men running his way. The two men had AR-15's and were shooting at Gino. Gino's body was being ripped apart, and all you saw was his blood splattering on the wall behind him. Gino dropped down to his knees. His guns fell right beside him. He looked up at one of the guys as blood was coming from his mouth. Both men stepped to the side as Lil John walked up to him with a shotgun in his hand.

"Look at you, Gino, you had Vinnie killed, now Fat Rob had you killed."

Lil John pointed the shotgun at Gino's face and pulled the trigger, blowing his face off. Lil John looked around. "Get the guys he killed and then set this bitch on fire." Lil John pulled out his phone and called Fat Rob. After two rings, Fat Rob picked up. "He's swimming with the fishes."

Lil John hung up the phone and walked out of Gino's house.

Chapter Thirty-Eight

Jamila sat in her office watching the news. The headlines read, "MAFIA KINGPIN GINO SABRANO ASSASSINATED". Jamila read on, taking in the part that said: *Last night he was found dead in his home with multiple gunshot wounds to his upper body and head. The fire department was called to a house fire where Mafia boss Gino Sabrano was dead inside.*

Jamila got up from her desk and went to the bar and poured a shot of gin and took it for Gino. She walked back to her desk and called Tasha to come to her office. She sat down and waited for Tasha to come in. With Gino dead Jamila knew hell was going to break loose. She needed to get to the bottom of it. Tasha walked through Jamila's door to her office.

"Tasha, last night Gino was murdered and I know for a fact it was the Lenacci family who did it. What I need for you to do is, go see Fat Rob and tell him we need to talk. Take Masi and Muscle with you."

"When do you want me to do this?" asked Tasha.

"Today, I need to know something asap. Let him know to come see me tomorrow no later than four p.m. I'll be here till then," said Jamila.

"Okay, Ms. LaCross. I'll go take care of that now."

Jamila nodded at Tasha then finished watching the news as they showed pictures of Gino's house and property.

***

"Iceman, shit is crazy," Perk G told him. "Did you see the news yet?"

"Yea, I did and that's crazy. Gino Sabrano got his head knocked off."

"What you think Symone is going to have to say about this?" asked Perk G.

"I don't know, Perk G. What I do know is that she fucked with him hard as hell and she might get on the bullshit now that he is dead. Here goes another bloody summer, the stories of our life. But look, here goes another ten kilos. When you think I can come pick the money up?" asked Perk G.

"Shit, give me about two weeks at the most. I'll give you a call then."

"Say less, homie."

Iceman dapped Perk G up as he left the casino.

Iceman looked at all the kilos on his office desk. He picked the bag up and walked to the closet and pulled the bags inside.

***

Agent Brooks knocked on Special Agent Carter's office door.

"Come in," replied Agent Carter.

"Sir, how are you today?"

"I'm fine, Agent Brooks, come in and have a seat and tell me what's on your mind."

Agent Brooks took a deep breath. "Sir, I want to put Agent Melissa back on the case. Her cover was never blown and now with Gino Sabrano dead we need to know what's going to happen next."

Special Agent Carter took off his glasses and placed them down on his desk. "Are you sure this is what you want to do? Because it's not your life that's on the line, it's hers. Are you sure you want to take that risk?"

"It's not my risk, it's hers to take."

"Did you talk to her about it already?" asked Agent Carter.

"She wants to talk to you about it; she's outside now," replied Brooks.

"Okay, go bring her in and let's talk."

Agent Brooks got up and walked to the door.

"Melissa, come inside."

Melissa walked into the office and took a seat in front of Special Agent Carter's desk.

"Hello, sir."

"How are you doing, Agent?" asked Agent Carter.

"Good, sir."

"So you want to be put back on the case?"
"Yes, sir"
"You do know that Agent Corey's cover was blown," said Carter
"Yes, I do know, sir, but Agent Corey was moving too fast. I was taking my time getting to know my target."
"That was smart of you to do. Okay, you want to go back in? Okay, you got it. I'm putting you back undercover."
"Thank you, sir, I will not let you down."
"I know you won't," replied Carter. "Brooks, I want eyes on her at all times."
"Yes, sir."
"Now I think you two have some work to get done."

***

Fat Rob walked into *Destiny's* with Lil John to the ballroom where Jamila and Tasha were waiting for him. Jamila stood up and walked to Fat Rob as he was walking through the doors.
"Fat Rob, thank you for coming to see me."
"It was not a problem, Queen don. So please tell me what this is about."
"Come have a seat and let's talk. Tasha, can you bring me a bottle of brandy to the table with two shot glasses, please?" asked Jamila.
Mr. Lenacci, about two weeks ago someone tried to kill Gino Sabrano with a car bomb.
Jamila stopped talking when she saw Tasha walking to the table with the bottle of brandy and two glasses.
"Thank you, Tasha."
"You're welcome, Ms. LaCross."
Tasha turned around and walked off back to the bar next to Lil John while Jamila and Fat Rob talked.
"Like I was saying, someone tried to kill him, now two weeks later he's killed in his own house and I believe by your own men," said Jamila

Saynomore

"And why do you say by my own men?" said Fat Rob.

"Because when I went to see him he told me that Vinnie tried to get Joey to kill him, so he killed Joey. Then a few days later he had Vinnie killed."

"When did you find this out, Ms. LaCross?"

"Two days ago he told me about him killing Vinnie after I told you I would look into it for you. Everything came to the light so now I'm asking you, Mr. Lenacci, did you have your hands in Gino's murder?"

Fat Rob looked at Jamila and took his shot of brandy.

"Yes, I had him killed for killing Vinnie—a murder for a murder, blood for blood."

Jamila took her shot of brandy then poured both of them another shot.

"So is it over now?" asked Jamila.

"Yes, it is."

"Good, now this conversation is just between me and you and I thank you for your honesty."

Both of them took their shot together for Vinnie and Gino. Fat Rob got up and gave Jamila a hug and a kiss on both cheeks before walking out the bar.

"So what did he say?"

"Everything I already knew, Tasha. Come on, we have to get back to *Jelani's*.

Chapter Thirty-Nine

Cindy walked into her new house and looked around.
"How do you like it, Ms. Morris?"
"It's beautiful."
"I'm glad you like it. Someone will be here to see you in the next few days to see how you are adjusting to the new location."
"Okay, thank you."
Cindy watched as both officers left to go back to NYC. She stepped outside her new house and looked around as she started to walk down the street. LA was her new home. And she knew it was only a matter of time before Symone found out where she lives and sent her goons to come get her. So she knew she needed to make friends, just in case she needed somewhere to hide out at. One thing she learned was: *When the Mob is after you there's no place to hide.*

***

Victorious walked into Jamila's house to the kitchen where Jamila was eating at the table.
"I see you are home early. How do you like the job?" asked Jamila.
"It's cool, matter of fact—the other day I was in the investigation room, Crystal was showing me around and I saw you and Symone's billboard with everyone's picture on it and you and Symone were at the top of the pyramids.
"So we are under investigation?" asked Jamila.
"No you are not, it's just in the investigation room."
"You see why I wanted you to work there now?"
"Yes, I do."
"Good, come to the garage, I have something for you in there," said Jamila.
Victorious walked into the garage and saw a black 2014 Cadillac SRX premium with 20' rims all black.
"Oh my God! This is for me?"

"Yes, it is, baby girl, and I talked with a few friends of mine. The problem you had in Long Island is over with. Nothing is going to come back to you."

Victorious turned around and hugged Jamila.

"Thank you so much, sis."

"No problem. I told you I got you, just do your part for me and Symone's family"

"I promise you I will, sis."

"I know you will, baby girl. When was the last time you talked to mom?"

"Three days ago. I might go see her this weekend," replied Victorious.

"Well, let me know if you do, okay?"

"I will."

"Now come on back inside and finish telling me about your job and what they have you doing there."

***

Symone leaned back in her seat as she smoked her *black and mild*, as she read the newspaper about Gino Sabrano's murder. She knew that Fat Rob was the one who had him killed. It wasn't hard to put two and two together. She had a choice to make to keep her word to Gino after his death or to leave it alone. That's when Halo walked into her office.

"I see you reading the newspaper."

"Yea, it's fucked up how Gino was killed, but the one question I'm asking myself is: Do I leave it alone or do I send my shooters at Fat Rob?"

"Symone, Gino Sabrano is dead so you don't have to honor your word to him any more. Why put the family at war if you don't have to?" replied Halo.

"You make a good point, Halo, you know what? Fuck it! It's over. So what brings you to my office?" asked Symone.

"I just got word back to me where Cindy Morris is staying at."

Symone got up and walked to her office window.

"Where did they relocate her to?"

"Sunny California. I know two families out there who might be able to help me out with that issue."

"What families?" asked Symone.

"The Savatos are the main family I'm talking about. Do you want me to reach out to them?" asked Halo.

"No, I will call them. Just find out where she stays and her new identity for me."

Halo nodded and walked off. Symone walked off down the stairs to her car.

"Slim Boogie, come take a ride with me."

"Where?"

"We going to see Red Invee. Halo, I'll be back in a few."

***

Pistol was talking to the bartender when he saw Kia walk through the doors.

"Josh, hold that thought. I'll be right back."

Pistol walked up to Kia before she could take a seat. She was looking good with her all-black outfit on and high heels.

"Where the fuck you been at?"

"Well, it's good to see you again, Pistol. Well, I've been upstate NY with my mother."

"You haven't seen none of the text messages I sent you back to back?"

"Yes, I saw them, I was just going through a lot. I'm sorry for not replying back to you, bae," replied Kia.

Now, I'm your bae?"

"You always were."

Pistol looked at Kia and grabbed her hand and led her to his office.

"You want something to drink?" asked Pistol.

"Yes please. I'll have a shot of Henny."

"With ice or without ice?"

"Without, so how have you been?" asked Kia.

"Good, just trying to run it up, that's all."
"That makes two of us."
"What you mean that makes two of us?" asked Pistol.
"You ain't the only one trying to get a bag."
"So now you are a bad girl?"
"I always have been."
"You know what? You funny as hell, Kia. So what you trapping?"
"Powder."
"I guess you could get your bag up with that. I don't deal with powder," said Pistol.
"What you hustle?"
Pistol looked at Kia and smiled as he walked to his desk and opened his desk drawer and pulled out a bundle of small packages and threw it to Kia.
"That's Red Flame, beautiful, and it flows like water throughout the city. Motherfuckers can't get enough of it."
Kia looked at the Red Flame. "How much for this?"
"Keep it, that's on me. Just bring me some new money. Each of them is fifty dollars apiece."
Kia got up, walked to Pistol and gave him a kiss on the lips.
"Hold on, baby girl." Pistol went and locked his office door and grabbed Kia. "Now, where were we?"
Kia smiled as she started to kiss Pistol again.

Chapter Forty

Detective Mayfield walked into the briefing room where special Agent Carter was at and Agent Brooks.

"Detective Mayfield, we have two big problems and I think you know what it is. We're not going to fool ourselves. DA Kendrick and Detective Hall have been missing for more than four weeks now and if I have to guess they are dead somewhere waiting for someone to find their bodies."

"And let me guess, you think Symone Rose is behind their disappearance, Mr. Carter."

"You took the words right out of my mouth, Detective Mayfield."

"So how do you plan on finding this information out?"

"We put Agent Melissa back in undercover in the Rose family."

"Agent Books, was Corey able to remember anything?" said Detective Mayfield.

"No, he said he never talked to nobody about the drugs or how they move before his cover was blown."

"Right now we are betting on Melissa; she already made a deal. She's with one of the Rose family members named Pistol, with the drug Red Flame. We just need to keep hoping that her cover is not blown," said Agent Carter.

"So how is she going to find out if the Rose family is responsible for the murder of Detective Hall and DA Kendrick? We just have to hope that someone opens their mouth about it. We don't want her to start asking questions."

"You are right, Mr. Carter."

"So we just wait for the right time to hit them where it will hurt the hardest. Once we find out where they keep the records at, then we are going in. What I do know is that Symone does own the docks now that used to be owned by the Teliono family.

"So what? You think she keeps the records there, Mayfield?"

"I don't know, sir, but what I do know is that whoever killed Gino Sabrano, their body will be floating in the Hudson soon."

Saynomore

"Look, let's focus on the main thing right now and that is Symone Rose. We got the buy money. If we get this Pistol on tape he might be the weakest link. So let's focus on him for now."

"Let's do this then, sir."

Chapter Forty-One

Victorious walked into *Destiny's* and sat at the back of the diner where she could work on her laptop and eat her food in peace. Crystal had been showing her the ropes from day one. She had two files she had to work on. She looked and saw Pistol walking out of the hotel with a female hand in hand. She got up and walked to the front of the diner just in time to see her get into a yellow cab. As the cab drove off, she knocked on the glass window to get Pistol's attention. He turned around and looked at her before walking back into the hotel to the diner where Victorious was at.

"What's up, beautiful?" asked Pistol.

"You tell me what's up, lover boy. I see you trying to creep up out of here, laughing out loud. Who was that you were with?" asked Victorious.

"Oh, baby girl, her name is Kia. I been rocking with her for a minute now. What you doing up in here?"

"Just trying to get some work done and getting something to eat at the same time."

"Well, look, baby girl, I have some runs to make, so won't you come by the club tonight and kick it with me?" said Pistol.

"You know what? I might do that."

"Cool, I'll see you then."

"Okay then."

Victorious turned around and walked back to her table. She ain't tell Pistol, but she knew she seen Kia somewhere before; she just don't know where.

***

"Gino is dead, Gino is dead. What are we going to do about it, Jamila?"

"Nothing, Symone."

Jamila looked at Symone and smiled.

"What are you smiling about?" asked Symone.

Saynomore

'Symone, this is the Mafia. Gino was killed because he had Vinnie killed, and it came back to him. We do not need a war on these streets. It's over, there is nothing we can do about it. For once our hands are clean of any of the bullshit. So let's keep it that way, Symone."

'You really think that, sis?"

"Do you know something I don't know, Symone?"

Jamila looked at Symone. "Symone, what have you done?"

Symone pulled out a *black and mild* and lit it.

"You want to know what I did? Gino came to see me one night, a few weeks ago. And told me how Vinnie paid Joey off to kill him, but it didn't work the way they planned. So he wanted Vinnie dead and he asked me to do it for him. So I had one of my guys make a fake phone call to talk with him about some new business. He bit the bait. I watched him get into the limo and I followed him all the way to NJ. Once he was by the exit to head into New Jersey, I called two of my guys who was waiting on him to reach that very spot. By the time it was over, Vinnie and Bull were dead to the world. Yea, I was the one who had him killed, but just not for Gino but for you too, over his disloyalty to you, Queen Don. After his death, Gino asked me to kill the rest of the family, but now that Gino is dead I said *fuck it*."

Jamila couldn't believe what she was hearing.

"Symone, who else knows this?" asked Jamila.

"Just Iceman and Pistol, no one else but you."

"Gino told me he had someone do it he trusted, but I never would have guessed it was you. Symone, it's over now, never speak of this again. Come on, we need to go to the docks."

"For what?" asked Symone.

"To clean up the water graves," said Jamila. Victorious told me that they have our pictures up still, so we need to clean up our tracks fast.

Symone nodded and followed Jamila out the doors to the limo to head to the docks.

***

Savato sat at his table eating a tomato, still reading the paper.

"Someone knows who killed Gino. His murder can't go unanswered."

"Who do you think killed him? What family pushed the button?" asked Jimmy.

"That I don't know, but I honestly think that Ms. LaCross may know something."

"So are we going to NYC?"

"Yea, we are, Jimmy."

"So when are we leaving?"

"Let's leave tonight after six p.m. Get a few guys together for the trip because we are not leaving till we take care of the person who killed Gino," said Savato.

"Yes, sir." Jimmy turned around and walked out of Mr. Savato's house. As he was walking out, Mr. Savato's phone went off. He looked at the unknown number before picking up the phone.

"Hello, Mr. Savato."

"Yes, this is him, who am I talking with?"

"Symone Rose."

"Ms. Rose, what can I do for you?" asked Savato.

"I have a little problem that relocated to California."

"And what is this problem?"

"Her name is Victoria Starks and she took the stand against me on trial."

"Now she's hiding out here in the witness protection program?"

"Yes, she is, Mr. Savato."

"I think I can take care of this problem. I'm coming to NY tonight so how about we can talk face to face because I also have a little problem you may be able to help me with, Rose," replied Savato.

"Just call my phone when you get here. I'll be waiting to hear from you," said Symone.

"Sure thing, Ms. Rose."

Savato hung up the phone and finished eating his tomato.

Chapter Forty-Two

Victorious walked into the strip club and sat at the bar as the females were dancing on stage to 50 Cent's "Candy Shop," when the bartender walked up to her.

"What can I get for the beautiful lady?"

Victorious looked at him with a smile.

"I'll have a rum and coke with ice."

"Coming right up, beautiful."

Victorious watched as the females gave lap dances to male and female customers. After getting her drink, she took a seat at the back of the club, bobbing her head to the music until she saw Pistol and Iceman walking to the VIP with Kia. Pistol was holding her hand. She thought about going up there, but she was enjoying herself where she was. She got up and started throwing five and ten dollars on stage as she was dancing to the music with them. One of the girls winked at Victorious as she went to take her seat.

"What's up? I never seen you here before, sexy," one of the dancers said to her.

"Because this is my first time here," replied Victorious.

"Okay, you like it so far?"

"Yea, it's cool. What's your name?"

"Honey and what's yours?"

"Victorious."

"So what made you come here tonight?" asked Honey.

"To see Pistol, but I see he has his hands full with that female he's with."

"You can say that again, she popped up out of nowhere, disappeared for a few months, now she's back. Shit, Pistol act like he don't know us no more."

"You know how niggas get."

"How do you know Pistol?" replied Honey.

"From my two older sisters," said Victorious.

"Oh your sisters are dancers here?"

"No," replied Victorious, "my sisters run NYC."

"And who are you sisters?" asked Honey as she raised her eyebrows.

Victorious took a sip of her drink then looked at Honey.

"Jamila LaCross and Symone Rose."

Honey looked at Victorious.

"Wait, you mean to tell me your sister owns this club?" asked Honey.

"Yea, she do."

"So why you ain't in VIP then?"

"Because I'm comfortable down here."

"Right."

Honey looked and saw Iceman coming out the office walking downstairs to the bar.

"There goes one of the bosses coming downstairs now. Go tell him that Victorious is in the club."

"Okay, beautiful, I'll be right back."

Victorious watched as Honey walked up to Iceman.

"Hey, handsome!" said Honey.

"What's good, Honey? How you doing tonight up in here? replied Iceman.

"I'm good. I'm over there chillin' with Victorious. She said she know you."

"Where she at?" asked Iceman.

Honey pointed to the back of the club. When Victorious saw her pointing her way, she waved to both of them.

"What the fuck she doing in here by herself?"

"I don't know," replied Honey, "she was throwing fives and ten dollars on stage when I met her."

"Shit! Come on, Honey."

"What's up, Iceman?" said Victorious as she got up to hug him.

"What's up, Vee? Why are you in here by yourself?" asked Iceman.

"Pistol told me to come through. I only been in here about an hour," replied Victorious.

"Do Pistol know you are here?"

"No, not yet."

Iceman looked around.

"Shit, come on, let's get you out of here."

"Okay, well, let me go say what's up to Pistol first?"

"He's taking care of some business right now. So you are going to have to make a rain check on that, Vee." Iceman looked at Honey and pulled out $1000 and handed it to her.

"Good looking out and taking care of baby girl."

"I wasn't taking care of her, we was just chilling," said Honey.

"Good looking anyway, Honey. Vee, come on, we out."

"Bye, Honey"

"Take care, Victorious."

"Iceman, why are we leaving?" asked Victorious.

"Because you don't need to be here, anything can happen at any moment. What car is yours?"

"That one over there."

"Damn, I see your sister got you driving nice. Give me your car keys, I'm driving," said Iceman.

"And where are you taking me?" asked Victorious.

"Home."

Victorious handed him the car keys.

"So why I couldn't go see Pistol?"

"He was taking care of business, plus I don't think your sister would like it if she knew you were around that kind of stuff right now."

"So if you are driving me home, how are you going to get back home or wherever?"

"Don't worry about me. I will be fine." Iceman pulled the car over a little way from Jamila's house.

"Look, go home and get some sleep."

"Okay, you sure you are going to be okay?" asked Victorious.

Iceman pointed to the car coming down the street. "I'm always going to be alright. That's one of my guys following me." Iceman turned around and walked to the car. He watched as Victorious drove off.

***

Jamila sat in the stadium listening to the female playing the violin when Tasha walked in.

"So were you able to find anything out?" asked Jamila.

"Yea, I was and what I was told was that we have a visitor coming to NY tonight," replied Tasha.

"And who is this visitor?"

"Savato."

"Wait, you telling me Savato is coming to NY."

"From what I was told, yes," replied Tasha.

"And who told you this?"

"Eddie from the Landon family told me this."

"Did he tell you the reason for his visit?" asked Jamila.

"Yea, he did, Gino Sabrano."

"So he's coming out here for answers to Gino's death. Did he say who he was coming to see?"

"No, he didn't," said Tasha.

"Don't you think you should find out?" replied Jamila.

"Yea, I should."

"Good, let me know something as soon as possible."

Tasha got up and walked away. Jamila never took her eyes off the female playing the violin as she thought about what was about to come her way. When the female stopped playing, Jamila stood up and started clapping for her.

***

"Victorious, could you meet me in the investigation room?"

"Sure, I'm on my way now, Crystal."

"Okay, bring the tax files when you come please?"

"Sure thing."

When Victorious walked into the room, she saw Crystal talking to a man from the 4th floor.

"Victorious, come meet Michael Stone. He's with the white-collar crimes department."

"Hello, Mr. Stone," said Victorious.

"How are you doing today, Ms. Moore?" replied Stone.

"I'm doing well."

"I see. Crystal told me how wonderful of a job you are doing here."

"She is a great teacher. She is showing me the ropes."

"Victorious, can I have the files I asked you to bring please?" asked Crystal.

"Sure, they are right here."

"Okay, give me a minute and I'll be right back with you. Let me show Mr. Stone a few things."

"Okay, I will be over there, Crystal," said Victorious as she walked to the billboard that Jamila and Symone's pictures were on. She looked at the photo under Symone's billboard. She was looking at the picture of Kia, that Pistol was hanging out with.

"Victorious, come on, we have to go to the fourth floor." said Crystal.

"Right behind you, Crystal." Victorious read Kia's name before walking off.

Chapter Forty-Three

Symone sat down at her desk as she waited for Iceman to bring Mr. Savato to her office. There was a knock on her door. As Iceman opened it up, Symone got up and walked to Mr. Savato.

"How was your trip, Mr. Savato?" asked Symone.

"Long, very long."

"Come in and please have a seat. Can I get you something to drink? Water, wine, or something stronger?"

"Yes, something stronger and something to eat if you can," replied Mr. Savato.

"Sure thing, Mr. Savato. Iceman, can you have the kitchen bring up something for Mr. Savato and his men please?"

"Yes, Ms. Rose," said Iceman.

"Mr. Savato, come tell me the nature of your visit while we wait for your food to come."

"Ms. Rose, I can't just roll over knowing that Gino Sabrano was gunned down in his own house. That just don't sit right with me. So, I came to New York to see what I can find out. I want to know who green-lighted the hit on Gino Sabrano."

"So Mr. Savato, where do you plan on looking first?" asked Symone.

"Honestly, I don't feel I have to look any further, Ms. Rose, I believe you can fill me in on what I need to know."

Symone reached in her desk drawer and pulled out a *black and mild* and lit it.

"Mr. Savato, do you respect the code of silence?" asked Symone.

"Yes I do. Why do you ask?"

"To make sure we are on the same page. So let's just say I do know something that can help you out with our line of questions. What would you do for me?"

"Ms. Rose, I have a lot of friends who think very highly of me. After our little phone conversation, I made a few calls and came across this name."

"What name?" asked Symone.

"Cindy Morris."

Mr. Savato snapped his fingers and one of his guys brought him a briefcase.

"Ms. Rose, you might want to take a look at these pictures. Symone looked at the pictures of Cindy Morris laying on the ground dead with her eyes open. Then she looked at the pictures of her chopped up. She handed the pictures back to Mr. Savato.

"I see you are a very forward man," replied Symone with a smile on her face.

"I am. So, now I ask you, Ms. Rose, what can you do for me?"

At that time there was a knock at the door.

"Come in." Symone watched as the food server came in with the food.

"Please place the food over there on the table. Mr. Savato, you asked me what I can do for you? First, I can feed you and your men. Then I can promise you your trip was not a waste of time. You will see it on the news or read about it in the paper."

Mr. Savato nodded at Symone as they sat down to eat their food with no more words to be said.

***

Pistol got in his car and was headed to see Kia. She told him the Red Flame was moving well and she wanted two kilos. He had both kilos in the car heading her way when his phone went off.

"Hello."

"Pistol, listen to me, whatever you are about to do, stop right now and go to a payphone and call me right back," said Victorious.

"Can this wait?" asked Pistol.

"No, do it now."

"Okay, give me two minutes." Pistol pulled over at the deli and walked inside. "Yo, let me get two breakfast sandwiches and let me use your phone real quick." The man handed the phone to Pistol and he walked down the aisle; he called Victorious.

"Yo, what's up, Vee?"

"Look, your little girlfriend Kia, she is an undercover officer and she's working one on you."

"Are you sure?" replied Pistol, curious.

"Yea, I am. I saw her picture on your case file."

"Shit, I was just about to sell her two kilos."

"Where are they now?" asked Victorious.

"In the deli. Let me take care of this and I'll call you back."

"Pistol, get rid of your phone before they get it."

"I'm doing that now." Pistol handed the man back the phone.

"How much I owe you for the food?" asked Pistol.

"Five dollars."

"Look, check me out, here goes a thousand dollars. Take this phone and flush it down the toilet and take my gun and hide it for me. I'll be right back."

Pistol walked to his car and came back with the black bag in his hand.

"I need to flush this now."

"Come on this way," replied the man.

Pistol walked into the bathroom and started flushing everything. After he was done, he poured bleach on everything. When he walked out the bathroom, there were two men at the counter. As he went to walk past the counter, the cashier stopped him. "Sir, your food."

"Oh yea, thank you."

Pistol looked at both men before walking out the deli. He looked around before getting into his car, driving off.

"Fuck, fuck, fuck that bitch. Shit. damn it."

Pistol drove to the strip club. It was clean. Nothing was in there. He needed to clear his head and to call Victorious back.

***

Styles walked up to Jamila and hugged her from the back as he kissed her neck. Jamila turned around and looked at Styles.

"You can't be spending all your time with me. Your wife is going to wonder who you spending all your time with. Only if she knew what I was doing with you, Styles."

"Jamila, where are we going and what are we doing with each other?"

"Styles, don't get it fucked up. All you are to me is a tongue and a dick, nothing more. Matter of fact, get dressed and get out of my office."

"Jamila."

Jamila looked at Styles and tilted her head. "What I say?" Jamila watched as Styles left her office. She walked to her bathroom in her office and closed the door so she can clean herself up.

***

Kia watched as Pistol pulled up to the parking lot. He stepped out of his car and walked up to her.

"Where have you been? I been calling you for hours," said Kia.

"Look," replied Pistol, "things ain't go the way I planned on my end."

"So what about our deal?"

"There is no deal. I got some shit I need to take care of."

"So that's it?" asked Kia.

Pistol turned around and looked at the van a little way down the parking lot then to the man and female sitting on the bench.

"You know, Kia, at one time I thought it was real."

"What are you talking about, Pistol?"

Pistol walked up to Kia and said in her ear. "I don't talk to cops."

'Rock and Roll, Rock and Roll, she's been made.'

Pistol watched as the van came speeding his way with four more other cars. "Freeze, don't move, don't move." Pistol put his hands in the air as the police officers ran up to him. They cuffed him up then went to search his car.

"Shit, he's clean, there's nothing here."

"Did he have anything on him, agent?"

"No, nothing"

Pistol was looking at the two men he saw at the deli earlier today walking around. He didn't say anything as he was placed in the back seat of the police car.

"Agent."

"Yes, sir."

"How do you think he found out?"

"I don't know."

"Sir?"

"Yea, Mark?"

"Today when we were following him he got a call on his phone then went to the deli. I think he got a call then. He made sure everything was clean before he came here, sir."

"Look, go hit the strip club and his house and let's see what we can come up with?"

"Yes, sir."

***

Halo walked into Symone's office. Symone looked at him and the expression on his face.

"What is it, Halo?"

"Ro just called me. We got the alphabet boys in the strip club shaking us down."

"Where is Pistol at?" asked Symone.

"They got him," replied Halo.

"Fuck! Okay, have Iceman head down there to check it out. Call the attorneys and see what they have on Pistol. Do you know if the place was cleaned?"

"Yea, everything is clean there, I know that for a fact."

"Good, find out what you can and let me know," said Symone.

"I'm on that now."

Symone walked to her desk and called Perk G to let him know what was going on.

***

Saynomore

Jamila walked up to Tasha in the lobby of *Jelani's* by the front door.

Tasha, can I have a word with you?"

"Sure, what's up, Ms. LaCross?"

"Come, Tasha, let's talk in your office," said Jamila.

Once in Tasha's office, Jamila closed the door.

"Tasha, were you able to find out who Mr. Savato was down here to see?"

"Yea, I did. I was coming to tell you earlier, but you had your office door locked."

"Who did he come to see?" asked Jamila.

"Symone, I was told."

Jamila shook her head.

"I need to talk with her now."

"That might be a little problem. She has the FBI raiding her strip club and one of her guys is locked up."

"How do you know this?"

"I got a call from Halo telling me this."

"What do they have?"

"Nothing as I know of right now."

"Okay, let me go make some calls and I'll be back in a few."

"Okay."

Jamila walked out of Tasha's office when her cell phone went off. "Hello."

"Hey, sis."

"Victorious, let me call you back. I have to call Symone."

"That's why I'm calling you. Earlier today I called Pistol and told him the female he's been seeing is an undercover agent and they are watching him now. I just left the breakroom and I saw they had him in handcuffs, but I overheard them say he's clean. They have nothing on him."

"Okay, that's good. Keep your phone by you. Let me call Symone and tell her."

"Okay, sis. I will."

Jamila hung up the phone and called Symone.

Chapter Forty-Four

Agent Brooks walked into the investigation room and took a seat right behind the desk.

"Pistol, we been watching you for a very long time. You know if we are tracking you then we have you dead to the wrong. So, this is the part of the conversation where you might want to start talking so we can cut a deal for yourself."

Pistol laughed in Agent Brooks' face.

"You got me fucked up all the way. Whatever you got on me, book me for it. I call your bluff, motherfucker."

Agent Brooks knocked two times on the desk then got up and walked away. As he stepped outside the door, Special Agent Carter walked up to him. "What we got, Brooks?"

"Nothing, sir. The club was clean, so was his car. He knew it was a set-up."

"Damn it, Brooks, do you know how this makes the department look?" asked Agent Carter.

"Nothing, just the packages of Red Flame he gave Agent Melissa, nothing else."

"Brooks, the only good thing I can say is both our agents are still alive. Cut him loose, there is no point to hold him. Have a report on my desk by tomorrow," replied Carter.

"Yes, sir."

Agent Brooks watched as Special Agent Carter walked away.

***

Symone picked up the phone and called Iceman; after a few seconds, he picked up.

"Hello."

"I want everyone on the docks tonight by eight p.m., every fucking one."

After saying that, she hung up the phone. Halo came walking into her office.

Saynomore

"Halo, I need you to go pick up Katrina and bring her to the docks tonight. We are having a meeting."

Symone got up and walked out the office to her limo that was outside waiting on her to take her to the docks. It was 7:45 p.m. Symone looked at everyone standing there.

"Pistol, you brought the Feds into my house after I told you to make sure she is who she says she is. I told you if she is not who she says she is, I was going to kill her, then I was going to kill you," said Symone angrily.

"Rose, I swear I ain't know."

"You know why I ain't going to kill you, Pistol? Because you have been loyal to me and our family, but you don't get a free pass at all. Fat Rob and Lil John need to die. You have forty-eight hours from tonight to do it. Let me say this now so everyone will have a clear understanding. If you bring the FEDS into my house, I will kill you and your family in the worst way. Iceman, you will run the strip club as well as the casino. Pistol, you will be in the background until things cool down for you. Perk G, how were things with the new shipment?"

"Good, I have the girls taking care of that right now, Ms. Rose."

"That's what I like to hear," replied Symone. I have nothing more to say. Pistol, forty-eight hours."

Symone was in her office smoking a *black 'n' mild* when Jamila walked in.

"Jamila, what a surprise! What do I owe the pleasure to this visit?"

Jamila looked at Symone then went and locked her office door. Symone watched as Jamila went and poured herself a shot of Cîroc then she went and sat down in front of Symone. Jamila looked dead into Symone's eyes. "Why did Mr. Savato come from LA to come talk to you?"

Symone took a deep breath and looked at Jamila then placed her *black 'n' mild* down.

"I owed him a blood oath?"

"And why is that?" asked Jamila.

Symone opened up her desk drawer and handed Jamila the pictures of Cindy Morris. Jamila sat quietly as she looked through all of them.

"What is the blood oath you owe to him?" asked Jamila.

"He wants Fat Rob and Lil John."

"What is the window you have to do this?"

"Seventy-two hours, he asked"

"You don't think the Feds are still watching you?" said Jamila. "Do you think this is smart?"

"I have to honor my end of the oath."

"That is true, but there are ways that you do things, Symone, and this is not the right way and I am telling you this. But I will promise you sis, you will learn."

Jamila got up and walked out of Symone's office, not looking back.

"You ready, Ms. LaCross?"

"Yes, Masi. Halo?"

"Yes, Ms. LaCross?"

"Watch out for my little sister."

"I will."

"Come on, Masi, we are leaving now."

***

"Lil John, come in, I need to eat. I feel like I'm losing weight here."

"Fat Rob, you don't have to worry about losing weight, it's all there, trust me," replied Lil John. "Where are we going to eat anyway?"

"The joint off of 42nd Street. The lasagna is to die for, wait until you taste it."

"So now that Gino is out the way, what are we going to do now?" asked Lil John.

"There is nothing for us to do. Don't nobody know what we did. The hit was successful, no heat came back on us, so things went beautiful if you ask me," replied Fat Rob. "Hey, hey, pull over in the front of the joint. I ain't trying to be walking around looking for the car when I'm done eating."

Pistol sat a few cars back as he watched Fat Rob and Lil John go into the restaurant. He got out of his car and looked around one more time before following them. When he reached the side of the restaurant, he saw Fat Rob's driver taking a piss on the side of the dumpster.

"Too many drinks, huh, I came to do the same thing," said Pistol.

Fat Rob's driver looked at Pistol in a disgusting way. "I don't drink or talk to your kind!" As he was walking past Pistol, Pistol pulled his gun out and smacked him in the back of the head, knocking him out cold. Pistol dragged him to the back of the alley and tied him up and put him in an old blanket to hide his body. He then walked back to the front of the restaurant and hid across the street next to a tree. He watched as Fat Rob and Lil John ate their food through the window in the restaurant. He saw when they got up from eating. He ran across the street and stood on the side of the building, gun in his hand.

"What I tell you, was not that a fucking plate of lasagna to die for? I mean bang right to the fucking head. It's that good, what I tell you," said Fat Rob. "What the fuck, Lil John, where the hell is the driver at? I mean like damn I told him to stay with the fucking car."

Pistol waited until they both turned around and walked up on them. When Fat Rob turned around, he saw Pistol as he was firing shots into his chest, dropping him to the ground. Lil John went to pull his gun out, but Pistol already shot him in the head, killing him. Pistol stood right over them, shooting them till his clip was empty. He looked around at both of them one last time and took off running back to his car.

***

Symone watched as big red words crossed her TV screen. BREAKING NEWS:

This is Barbara Smith with Channel 5 eyewitness news downtown Brooklyn on 42nd Street. Mafia boss Fat Rob was gunned down with one of his men outside of the Moon Lite restaurant. Both men were shot multiple times to the upper body. We do have one witness who said there was a man with a black hooded sweater who shot them here. Afterwards he took off running down the block.

Symone cut her TV off after seeing that brief newscast. She got up and walked to her bar and poured herself a shot of Cîroc, knowing she fulfilled her part of the agreement to her blood oath.

***

Crystal walked into the break room along with Victorious. You had special Agent Cater standing at the front of the room. His facial expression was pissed off.

"I'll get right to the point, for the next eight hours this break room is your office. There is a mole in the department and we are going to find it. Agent Seamore is going to go around with a Ziploc bag and a pen and paper. You will write your name on the paper and place your phone in the bag along with your car keys. If you refuse to do so, you will be taken into custody and charged with interfering with a police investigation and prosecuted to the highest degree of the law."

Crystal watched as Agent Seamore walked up to everyone with the Ziploc bag, taking everyone's phone and car keys. Crystal wrote her name on the paper and placed her phone and car keys in the bag. When Victorious went to do the same thing, Special Agent Carter stopped her.

"Not you. You are the new intern, right?" asked Carter.

"Yes, sir," replied Victorious.

"Well, you can leave for the day. Agent Seamore, can you see her out please?"

Victorious looked at Crystal as she got up and was taken out. Victorious walked to her car and saw Agent Melissa getting into a black 2-door Ford. She watched as she drove off, and followed her to a red brick house. Victorious watched as she got out of the car and walked into the house. "Victorious, you can do this. She tried to set your sisters up. You have to do this. Red Invee or Rose wouldn't second guess this choice. Victorious, come on, you are doing this now," she said to herself, knowing she knew what needed to be done.

***

"Hey, Corey, the things from the station you asked me to get, I have them."

So how long do we have to stay in this place?" asked Agent Melissa.

"I don't know, Melissa. Until Carter relocates us it might be two weeks at the most."

"Corey, are you expecting company?" asked Melissa.

"No way," replied Corey.

"Because there is someone at the door."

"Okay, I'm about to go see who it is, Melissa."

Corey walked to the door and opened it. "Can I help you?"

"I'm sorry. I was looking for my friend Kim," said Victorious.

"I'm sorry, she don't live here."

"Alright, sorry."

"Who is it, Corey?' asked Melissa.

When Corey turned his head, Victorious pulled her gun out and pointed it at Corey's head and pulled the trigger, blowing his head off, his body hitting the ground. Victorious ran into the house after Melissa, but Melissa grabbed her gun and shot two times at Victorious, making her duck inside the house. Melissa looked out the door and took off running outside, not noticing Victorious behind the door. Once Melissa ran outside, Victorious came from behind the door and shot her two times in the back.

Victorious walked outside and pointed the gun at Melissa's head. With blood coming from Melissa's mouth she looked up at Victorious.

"Who are you?"

"It don't matter."

Victorious pulled the trigger, shooting Melissa in the head, killing her. Victorious ran to her car, got in and drove off, leaving both bodies there with the front door open.

Saynomore

Chapter Forty-Five

"Come in and have a seat. Did anyone follow you?"

"No."

"Good, everyone is in the back."

Deadeye walked Connelly Gambino in the back room where everyone was sitting.

"Now that Mr. Gambino is here. I'mma get right to the point. Symone Rose needs to die. We all know she is the one who had Fat Rob and Lil John killed."

"Deadeye, how do we know this?"

"Why else would Lenny Savato come from the city of Angels to NY to see Rose, Connelly?" replied Deadeye.

"Rose hides her hand in the shadows, but she is not going to get away with it. This time. I would like to introduce everyone here to a close friend of mine. Everyone looked at the tall skinny man with the full beard and top hat on.

"Everyone, meet Carson Praise. He has a special gift of making people disappear. But in this case we are going to leave Symone Rose lying dead where she stands. All in favor of this say, Aye."

Deadeye looked at everyone from the Lenacci family, Gambino family, Landon family, Scott family and Teliono family raised their hands.

"Don't you think she is going to want blood for her blood, Deadeye?"

"Red Invee respects the way of the mob. So I say this too, let's just cross that bridge when we get there."

Everyone looked at each other and nodded.

"It's agreed then. Symone Rose dies.

***

"Detective Mayfield, it's two friendlies."

"Cause of death?"

"Gunshot wounds to the head."

"Shit, come on, let me see," replied Mayfield.

Saynomore

When the officer pulled the white sheets back, Detective Mayfield kneeled down and looked at the body outside in the front yard.

"Fuck me, shit. Let me guess, officer, the body in the house—white male, black hair?"

"Yes, sir."

"I have to go call this in now."

Detective Mayfield pulled his phone out and called Agent Brooks.

"Hey, Mayfield, what's up? I'm kinda busy right now."

"Two of my officers was called to a 187 in the Flatbush and when I get here it's two undercover agents," said Mayfield.

"What? You mean my two undercover agents?" replied Agent Brooks.

"The agents who were working the Rose and LaCross case are here dead, Brooks. They got the call a little bit under an hour ago, Brooks."

"Okay, I'm on my way there now."

"Okay, I'll be here when you get here, Brooks."

Detective Mayfield hung up the phone and walked to his police car as he waited for Brooks to show up.

Chapter Forty-Six

Muscle walked up to Masi smoking a blunt at the waste plant.

"What's good, homie?" said Muscle.

"Shit. Muscle, just putting up the rest of the shipment."

"You heard about Fat Rob and Lil John?"

"Yea, that shit is crazy bro, but guess who else got smoked, Masi?"

"Who? D.C., swear?"

"Dead ass head blown off, the shit was on the news this morning."

"There's too much shit going down in the city. They know who did it, Muscle?" asked Masi.

"Not a soul. Red Invee called me into her office today about it to see what I knew or heard. You think Rose got her hands in this shit?"

"It's not that, Masi, she just don't give no fucks like she can't be touched."

"Shittin' me, Muscle. Remember when she got laid out. She knows she can be touched, big facts."

"How much more do you have to put up?" asked Muscle.

"Shit, I just got done when you walked up."

"Shit, let's roll out then. I'm hungry as fuck, fam."

"Come on, we're out then, Muscle."

***

Jamila walked into the kitchen and saw Victorious eating at the table.

"Victorious, why you ain't at work?" asked Jamila as she was making herself a cup of coffee.

"They have a big investigation going on right now and they don't want no interns there right now," said Victorious.

"Damn, I need to talk to Crystal."

"It's not a good time right now, sis."

"Do you know how long the investigation is going to be going on?" asked Jamila.

"If so they didn't tell me."

"Victorious, you been watching the news all morning?"

"Yes, I have been," replied Victorious.

"What are they saying about the dead officers?"

"They are still looking for a suspect, but they are not going to find one."

Jamila looked into Victorious' eyes. Victorious cut her eyes away from Jamila.

"What you know that you are not telling me and don't lie?" said Jamila. "Remember the rules we went over."

Victorious let out a deep breath then looked at Jamila.

"I was the one who killed them yesterday afternoon at the house."

"Victorious, tell me you are lying?"

"No, I'm not. I found out where they was and I did what you and Symone would have done."

"Victorious, I don't need you running around killing people. We have guys for that. I told you the role I want you to play. Anyways, let me get Rose on the line. Do not leave the house."

"Wait, where is the gun at?"

"I wiped it down and threw it in the Hudson River," said Victorious.

"Okay, that was smart."

Jamila walked out the kitchen to the living room to get her phone to call Symone.

Jamila walked the living room floor until Symone picked up the phone. "Hello."

"We have a problem, Symone."

"What now?"

"I can't talk over the phone. Can you meet me at the docks?' asked Jamila.

"Yea, what time?"

"I'm on my way there now," replied Jamila.

"Okay, I will be there when you get there."

Jamila hung up the phone and walked back into the kitchen. "Go get dressed, Victorious, we are going for a ride."

***

Tasha was in her office when one of the waiters knocked on the door. "Come in."

"Excuse me, Tasha, we have a Detective Mayfield here to see Ms. LaCross."

"Where.s he at?" asked Tasha.

"At the front desk."

Tasha looked out her office door and saw him.

"Okay, go bring him to me."

"Okay."

Tasha went and sat back behind her desk and waited for Detective Mayfield to come to her office.

"Hello, Detective."

"Hello, Tasha."

"Please come in and have a seat."

"Thank you."

"So tell me, Detective. What can I do for you?" asked Tasha.

"I was actually looking for Jamila LaCross."

"I'm sorry she isn't here for the day. Is there something I can help you out with?"

"No, you can't, but can I ask you something?" said Detective Mayfield.

"Sure, what is it?"

"How does a Lt. at a prison become Jamila LaCross manager at one of her restaurants?" asked Mayfield.

Tasha just looked at him when he said that.

"You know I remember reading about an inmate who was stabbed to death at the prison you used to work at."

"What was her name?" asked Tasha.

"Kim, yea, that was it. She was a Northside Misses. She was stabbed to death early in the morning on the stairwell on the same

Saynomore

block you were working. And from the rumors it was by Jamila La-Cross, but unfortunately the knife was never found and there weren't any cameras by that stairwell. Two weeks before Jamila's release you quit your job and now you work here for her. One thing I can say about Jamila—NYC will never see another female Don like her ever again. Have a nice day, Tasha LaCross."

Tasha watched as Detective Mayfield walked out of the restaurant to his car. Tasha walked back to her office and picked up her phone and called Jamila, but she ain't pick up. She looked and saw that Detective Mayfield left his card on her desk. She put it in her desk drawer and walked out of her office.

***

Jamila opened the car door and stepped out. She waited for Victorious to get out of the car. She looked at her. "Come on, Rose is waiting on us."

When they reached the loading docks, they saw Symone standing there talking to Halo smoking a *black 'n' mild*.

"Halo, let me go talk with my sisters."

"Sure, I'll go look over the books. I'll be upstairs in the office if you need me."

Jamila and Victorious walked up to Symone.

"Our little sister is starting to act like you when you first came into the family."

"Jamila, what are you talking about?"

Jamila handed Symone the newspaper she had in her hand. Symone opened the paper and read the headline: UNDERCOVER OFFICER DEAD AT SAFE HOUSE. Symone looked at Victorious then Jamila.

"Does anybody else know?"

"Nobody, just us three," replied Jamila.

"How did you find out where they was at, Victorious?" asked Symone.

"I saw when Kia was leaving the station and I followed her to the house they was at."

"Where is the gun at, Victorious?"

"In the Hudson"

"Jamila, her mind is made up. I remember I was the same way, it's in her blood. The question is, where do we go from here?" asked Symone.

"I don't know, Symone. Victorious, what was you thinking about when you did what you did?"

"I said to myself, what would Jamila or Symone do?"

Jamila turned around and walked back to her car.

"Victorious, come on upstairs so we can talk."

Saynomore

Chapter Forty-Seven

Jamila walked into *Jelani's office*. Before she could sit down, Tasha walked in behind her.

"Red Invee, we have a problem."

Jamila turned around and looked at her. "And what is the problem that we have?"

"We had a Detective Mayfield come by today asking to speak with you. Then when I tell him you are not here he starts talking about the inmate Kim who was killed at the prison I used to work at."

"Did he leave a card?"

"Yes he did." Tasha handed Jamila the Detective's card.

"Was he by himself?" asked Jamila.

"Yea, he was.

"Okay, don't worry about him. I'll take care of him."

"Just keep the floor running good for me."

Tasha walked out of the office. Jamila picked up the phone and called Detective Mayfield.

"Detective Mayfield speaking."

"Hello, Detective."

"May I ask who I am speaking to?"

"Jamila LaCross."

"Ms. LaCross, I came by the restaurant looking for you today," replied Detective Mayfield.

"I know. I got your message. I'm here now if you need to see me."

"Sure thing. I'll be down there in thirty minutes."

"I'll be waiting for you to get here," said Jamila.

"I'll see you soon."

Jamila hung her phone up and turned the TV on the news to see what they were talking about with the two dead officers.

***

Saynomore

Jamila sat quietly behind her desk as Tasha walked Detective Mayfield into her office.

"Thank you for bringing Detective Mayfield to my office, Tasha."

"Is there anything else you need, Ms. LaCross."

"No, that will be all, Tasha." Jamila watched as Tasha walked out her office, closing the door behind her.

"Detective Mayfield, please come in and have a seat."

Jamila watched as Detective Mayfield took his seat in front of her desk.

"Now tell me, Detective, what can I do for you?" asked Jamila.

"Jamila, I'm not going to cut no corners. Shit is getting out of hand. Now we have two dead officers that were undercover in you and Symone's family."

"Detective, I know nothing about what happened to the two peace officers. I only know what I heard on the news about them."

"Jamila, let's not sugar-coat this. Since your name came up, there have been more bodies in New York city than ever before," said Mayfield angrily.

"Detective, I have nothing to do with that, but my one question is this, what can I do for you because I don't like talking about the past."

"You are leaving a blueprint and the next time I see you or your sister Symone, I'll be putting cuffs on you. I'm not scared of you or your sister Symone. The rest of these sons of bitches might be scared of you, but I'm not."

"*Sons of bitches* is how you address people, Detective. Let me clarify something for you, I'm a business woman, nothing more. Now I'm sorry for your losses, but you know what they say, sunrises are beautiful, but sunsets teach us that even endings can be beautiful. If you come to my restaurant looking for sympathy, it's in the dictionary between shit and syphilis!" said Jamila.

"I see you like street justice. I guess it works best for your kind, Ms. LaCross."

"A Queen must always protect her Queendom, Detective Mayfield."

"I will be seeing you around, Red Invee."

"I hope so, Detective, I feel safe when I have an officer of the law around me."

"I guess that's why Tasha quit and came to work for you. I guess this place is a lot better than a prison. Take care, Ms. LaCross."

"You too, Detective. I hope I was helpful." Jamila watched as he left her office. She picked up the phone and called Tasha to let her know to see Detective Mayfield out the restaurant and to come to her office. When Tasha walked in the office, Jamila put her finger up to her mouth to tell her to be quiet. Jamila walked around her desk and picked up the chair that Detective Mayfield was in and pointed to the wire that Detective Mayfield planted there on the low. Tasha just shook her head. Jamila nodded at Tasha and said *ready* without saying a word.

"Tasha, did you see Detective Mayfield to his car?"

"Yes, Ms. LaCross I did. Is everything alright?"

"Yes, everything is alright. Detective Mayfield is just looking for a reason to open a case against me," replied Jamila.

"Do you want me to call the lawyers to let them know you are being harassed by this detective?"

"No, that will not be necessary, Tasha. We are clean, all business is set. Just keep running the floor and if I need you I will call you."

"Alright, you know where I'm at if you need me."

Tasha walked out of Jamila's office. Jamila placed the chair on the table and walked out her office door, locking it.

Saynomore

Chapter Forty-Eight

"Rebecca, this is not the time nor place for this. I really need you to leave before things get out of hand."

"No, Styles, who are you fucking here? What bitch is it? Tell me."

"I'm not fucking nobody, Rebecca, you are tripping," replied Styles.

Jamila walked to the back of the restaurant where she saw her employees standing at the back door crowded.

"Why are ya at this door and not working?"

Everyone heard Jamila's voice. They walked away from the back door and went back to work.

"Styles, you know what? Fuck you and whatever bitch you are fucking up in this place."

"Rebecca, I told you I'm not fucking no one."

"So why you come home smelling like pussy then jump in the shower and put your clothes in the washer then, Styles?"

Jamila walked out the back door to where Styles and Rebecca were arguing.

"Excuse me, Styles and Misses, can you two please take this somewhere else. This is a place of business we are running here."

Before Styles could say anything, Rebecca looked at Jamila. "Can you mind your motherfucking business!"

"Styles, I'm walking back inside. When I come back out here, have this over with," said Jamila.

"You don't have to go nowhere. I'll leave when I get ready."

Jamila looked at Styles then walked up to Rebecca as she was pulling out her gun. Rebecca jumped back when she saw the gun.

"What's all that shit you was talking now, bitch?" said Jamila with blood in her eyes. "Now you listen to me, you ghetto hood rat bitch. You must not know who the fuck I am, I'm Red Invee, bitch. And let me tell you something. I been fucking Styles, no—let me correct myself, he's been eating my pussy and I just started letting him fuck me."

Rebecca looked at Styles and he just lowered his head.

"So now you know, bitch. Now here's your choice, you can leave by your own free will or I can have your ass carried out of here. And next time you come here, Rebecca, you ain't leaving."

Rebecca went to walk to her car. "Hold on, Rebecca." She stopped and looked at Jamila. "Take Styles with you. Styles, you are fired." Jamila turned around and went back into the restaurant.

"The next person I see not working is fired."

Jamila walked off to her office.

***

"Victorious, listen, baby girl, Jamila just wants you to be clean right now until the right time. Trust me, she knows what's best for you just like she did with me. She's not going to tell you nothing wrong."

"I know. I just thought I was doing the right thing by taking care of the business for you too. I just wanted to make you proud of me."

"We are proud of you, beautiful, very proud of you and we know you can take care of yourself. Now this really proves it," replied Symone.

"So where do we go from here, Symone?"

"You are going back to Jamila's house and keep doing what you are doing. Think about this, you got a nice ass truck, pockets overflowing with money, you are a made female. Just relax back, girl, ok?"

"Okay, sis," replied Victorious.

"Come on, let's get you home."

Victorious got up and gave Symone a hug before walking downstairs to where the limo was at.

"Iceman, take my sister to Jamila's house then come back here," said Symone.

"Yes, Ms. Rose. Come on, little one, let's get you home."

When Victorious got into the limo, she sat in the back and looked out the window.

"Lil one, trust me, things are going to work out for you," said Iceman.

"I don't want to work at the FED building. I want to work at one of the clubs. I want to be around my sisters," exclaimed Victorious.

"That time is going to come. You have to learn to walk before you run, lil one. I been down with your sister from day one. I'm her hitta and she's my rider. Trust me, shit is going to work out."

"I trust you, Iceman."

"I know you do."

***

"Halo, what time do the show start?"

"Seven o'clock and I already have me, you and Slim Boogie seats reserved for us."

"Good, come on, I don't want to be late."

"Symone, I don't know how I let you talk me into going to see *Cats*. I don't do Broadway plays."

"Slim Boogie, it's a first time for everything, plus I think you will like it."

"How long is this show?" asked Slim Boogie.

"Three hours, Slim Boogie, now come on, I don't want to be late at all." Symone walked to the limo and Halo opened up the backdoor to let her inside.

"Symone, I didn't even know you liked Broadway plays."

"I don't, Halo, I just thought it will be something new. We will try, that's all. And if we don't like it, we can always say we went to one before. Plus, it's about time we start doing new things. We need to meet new people; that means we have to start doing things that we weren't doing before."

When the limo pulled up in front of the theater, Slim Boogie got out and opened up the limo door for Symone to get out. Symone stepped out of the limo looking like she was going to the Oscars on the red carpet in her all-black dress and open-toe shoes. Her hair was in a bun; she looked outstanding. Halo and Slim Boogie walked her to their private seats. Symone sat quietly as the show began.

Saynomore

***

Pistol walked into the casino to Iceman's office. Iceman was drinking a glass of brandy when Pistol walked through the doors to his office.

"What's up, fam? You good?"

"Iceman, I keep thinking how I almost let that bitch set me up," replied Pistol.

"Bro, that shit is over with, plus shorty is swimming with the fishes as of yesterday."

"I don't give a fuck that she is dead. I'm mad at the fact I could have taken us all down."

"But you didn't; that's the point, so we good, bro," said Iceman.

"Yea, I guess you right. How things here tonight?" asked Pistol.

"Smooth like always. You know how it goes. Motherfuckers lose money on the tables, tricking off on females and buying the Red Flame. Look, Pistol, I know you want the strip club back, but right now you hot. Plus, we ain't doing no moves out of that spot right now. Just bitches dancing is all Symone wants out of there right now. Matter of fact, come have a drink with me."

"Iceman, so who took shorty out anyway?" asked Pistol.

"You ready for this one, homie?" Iceman gave Pistol his drink with a smile on his face. Pistol took his sip with a smile on his face. "Vee".

"Stop lying, homie."

"Dead ass baby girl is just like her two older sisters, a cold-hearted bitch. Word is she followed them then laid them down," replied Iceman.

"Damn, they whole bloodline is raw."

"But look, Pistol, I have to go do my walk on the floor, my rounds. You walking with me or you posting up here?"

"Shit, I'm walking with you."

"Come on then, Pistol."

***

Symone stood up with the rest of the people in the theater and started clapping.

"Halo, Slim, now tell me that wasn't a beautiful play."

"Symone, it was alright, but I will be damn if I come to another play like this ever again in my life."

"Slim Boogie, you just don't get it, that's why. What about you Halo?"

"It was nice. I understand the play. I saw the meaning of it."

Symone smiled as she held on to Slim Boogie and Halo arms as they walked her to the limo out front. "I can't believe it's raining out here, damn!" said Symone.

Slim Boogie, Halo, and Symone waited in front of the theater for the limo to pull up. No one saw the tall skinny man step out of the crowd. As he raised his gun, Symone had a smile on her face as she looked at Halo. Her smile turned into a frown when she saw the gun pointed at her. In a blink of an eye Symone watched as the bullets left the gun and hit her in the chest. By the time Slim Boogie and Halo turned around, their bodies were already dropping to the ground. The man ran up to Symone and shot her two more times in the chest before he walked off. Halo was shot in the neck and one of the bullets hit Slim Boogie in the head. People were screaming and running for cover as all three of them laid there in the front of the theater covered in blood in the rain.

Saynomore

Chapter Forty-Nine

Jamila was laying in her bed when her phone went off. She rolled over and saw it was Masi calling her. She looked at the time; it was 11:45 p.m.

"Masi, do you know what time it is?"

"Yea, and my bad for calling you this late, but I got some bad news for you."

"And what is it, Masi?" asked Jamila.

Masi took a deep breath before talking.

"Symone got shot tonight. Halo and Slim Boogie are dead, and Symone is in ICU. They don't think she going to make it. Iceman and Pistol are up at the hospital now, they just called me."

"Masi, what hospital?" asked Jamila.

"Southside."

"You and Muscle meet me up there right now."

Jamila hung up the phone, got up and put a jogger suit on and ran out the door to her car. She was at the hospital within thirty minutes. She parked in the front of the entrance doors and ran inside.

"Iceman, what happened?"

"I don't know all the details yet. From what I was told, they didn't even see it coming. Halo got shot in the neck and Slim Boogie in the head. And Symone got shot three times in the chest. They don't think she's going to make it. She's in surgery right now. She been in there for two hours now."

Jamila looked at the front doors and saw Masi and Muscle walk into the hospital.

"Where is she at, Pistol?"

"On the third floor."

"Masi, walk with me. Muscle, go park my car, come on ya now." When Jamila made it to the 3rd floor, she saw the doctor coming out of the surgery room.

"Excuse me, doctor, my name is Jamila LaCross. I'm Symone Rose's sister, how is she?"

"Do you want to go somewhere and talk, Ms. LaCross?" asked the doctor.

"No, we can talk here."

"Not good. I don't know if she is going to make it. She lost a lot of blood and we just got the bleeding stopped. She was shot three times in the chest. One of the bullets we couldn't even remove."

"Doctor, what are the chances of her making it?" asked Jamila.

"Under twenty percent. Like I said, it don't look good."

"Can I see her?"

The doctor looked around. "Yea, only you. Come on, I'll take you to her."

When Jamila walked into ICU, she saw Symone with tubes down her throat and IV's in her arm. She couldn't help but have tears in her eyes looking at her little sister. She walked up to Symone.

"Symone, I don't know if you can hear me. I'm here, sis, for you, I promise you. But I need you to fight for me. I need you to fight, baby girl. I know you can beat this, please fight, please."

Jamila looked at Symone as a tear rolled down her face. Jamila took her hand and wiped the tear off of Symone's face.

"Ms. LaCross, we have to go, your sister needs her rest," said the doctor

Jamila kissed Symone's forehead before leaving.

"Doctor, what is your name?"

"Doctor Peterson."

"Doctor, do you know who I am?" asked Jamila.

"Yes, I do."

"Save her life and I have one million dollars for you. Please save my sister's life."

"I'll do my best."

"Here, this is my number, call me if anything changes."

Jamila walked out to the hallway and looked at everyone.

"Pistol, Muscle, you are on guard duty. Don't leave this door at all. Don't give a fuck who tell you to move. Do I make myself clear?"

"Yes, Ms. LaCross."

"After twelve hours, Iceman, you and Masi switch shifts with them. I'll have to find out who did this to my sister."

***

Jamila walked into her house, she placed her guns on the living room table then walked to Victorious' room. She watched her as she was sleeping. She walked over to the bed and sat down next to her.

"Wake up, beautiful?"

Victorious sat up and rubbed her eyes.

"Hey, big sis, what's up? What time is it?"

"It's two a.m., baby."

"What's wrong, sis?" asked Victorious.

"I just left the hospital. Symone's been shot three times. They don't know if she's going to make it." Victorious covered her mouth as tears filled her eyes.

"Can you take me to see her?"

"Tomorrow, I will," replied Jamila.

"Who shot her?"

"I don't know, but I'll find out and when I do they're dead. Get some sleep and you are coming with me in the morning."

Jamila leaned over and kissed Victorious on the forehead before getting up and walked out her room.

Chapter Fifty

Jamila sat in her office watching the news they were talking about Symone Rose being shot. She been on the phone all morning calling around trying to see who called the hit on Symone Rose. But every phone call led to a dead end, nobody knew anything.

Tasha walked into her office and sat down in front of her desk.

"How is it going?"

"I called every family this morning and nobody knows anything," replied Jamila.

"Do you believe it?" asked Tasha.

"Not one person I talked to is believeable. Somebody knows something. They are just keeping it a secret from me. They trying to cover they tracks, that's all."

"Did you take Victorious to see her yet?"

"Yea, this morning I did. She broke down when she saw her like that," said Jamila.

"How is Symone's condition?"

"Not better. I'm starting to face the facts that my little sister is going to die." When Jamila said that, tears started coming down her face.

"Tasha, I'm going to kill them. I swear to God I'm going to kill all them motherfuckers when I find out who did this to my little sister!" said Jamila with rage in her eyes.

"Where is Victorious at now?" asked Tasha.

"At the house. I have her being watched twenty-four hours until I clear my head up."

"What about your mother?"

"When I got up there this morning she was already sitting at her bedside reading the bible to her."

Jamila's phone went off with an unknown number.

"Hold on, Tasha."

"Hello. Who am I speaking with?" asked Jamila.

"A friend. Can you meet me under the bridge on 124th Street within the hour?"

"I'm on my way there now."

Saynomore

Jamila hung up the phone.
"Come ride with me, Tasha. We need to go now."
Jamila pulled both her guns out from her desk drawer and made her way to the back door where her limo was waiting.

***

Savato sat down smoking his cigar, watching the news. The headlines read: *Symone Rose Fights For Her Life.*
"I see you are still watching the news, Mr. Savato."
"I am, Pete. I don't know who called this hit on Symone Rose, but I really don't think they know what they did," replied Mr. Savato.
"Jamila been making calls all morning. She called me asking questions, but I had no answers for her. So I guess all hell is going to break lose," said Pete.
"That's an understatement, Pete, hold on, they have an update on her condition," replied Savato.
This is Barbara Smith with Channel 5 action news. I'm at Southside hospital for y'all who is turning in last night, Symone Rose was shot with two of her men. Both of her guards were pronounced dead on the scene. Symone Rose was taken to the hospital with three gunshot wounds to her chest. For ya who don't know who Symone Rose is, the people of Brooklyn call her their Angel. She is known for helping the people out with school supplies for the children, helping pay rent and putting food on their tables. She has thrown fairs for the community and made sure every family in Brooklyn had a white Christmas. She is also known for taking pictures with the children. She promised to support all families. If you look behind me, you will see the many people holding up signs. You have signs that say: "God, please don't take away our angel," hold on, I just got an update. To the people of Brooklyn, NY I'm sorry to say, but Symone Rose didn't make it. She passed away ten minutes ago. This is a sad day for NYC."
"Symone Rose is dead." Savato walked to his bar and poured him and Pete two shots of gin for Symone Rose.

"Pete, let everyone know to stay out of NYC. This is about to be a bloody war; I can promise you that. A lot of people are going to fall."

***

Jamila sat under the bridge with Tasha when her phone went off.

"Hello, Ms. LaCross."

"Yes, this is her."

"Hello, this is Doctor Peterson. I'm sorry to tell you, but Symone passed away ten minutes ago."

A tear rolled out of Jamila's eye.

"Thank you, doctor, for all you have done," replied Jamila.

"I'm sorry, I wish I could have done more."

"It's okay, you tried your best."

Jamila hung up the phone.

"I'm sorry, Jamila."

"Thank you, Tasha."

Jamila opened up the limo door when she saw a man walking her way. She waited as he got in.

"Steve, it's been years. Why didn't you tell me it was you over the phone?" asked Jamila.

"Because, I don't know who to trust nowadays."

"What did you want to talk to me about?"

"Last night I was with a few guys at the pool hall and I overheard them say the hit on Symone Rose went down."

"Who said that?" asked Jamila.

"Leo Gambino, but that's not all. All the families came together and voted on her death."

"Are you sure?"

"Yes, I am. I have one more thing for you. The name of the man who killed her is Carson Praise," said Leo. "He's tall and skinny," Leo added.

Jamila had hate in her eyes when she looked at Tasha.

"I have to go, Queen Don," said Steve.

"Thank you, Steve. If you need anything, please come see me," replied Jamila.

"I will."

Jamila watched as Steve got out of her limo. She told the driver to take her to *Jelani's*.

"Tasha, call everyone from the Rose family and ours. I want them all at the restaurant by two p.m. today."

Chapter Fifty-One

Jamila looked at everyone sitting at the table to the Rose family.

"I am sorry for your loss. I know how much Symone Rose meant to you all. I called you all here because her death is not going to go unanswered. I know who killed her and I also know who green-lighted the hit on her life. But before we get to that, we need to talk about the Rose family. Now that Symone is gone, who will be the head of the family? Her family name will not die."

Iceman stood up.

"Ms. LaCross, it's not our family name, it's your family name." Iceman looked at everyone at the table. "I think the head of the family should be Victorious, that's what Symone would want. She told me she was going to make Victorious her number two."

Jamila looked at everyone at the table.

"Does anybody have anything to say?"

Nobody said anything.

"Okay then it's done. Iceman, you will be her number two, you will show her the ropes and everything she needs to know. Now that's said and done, after Symone's funeral, we are going to kill everyone with one stone. I'm going to call a meeting with the heads of every family and I'll tell them to bring two witnesses that's going to be they second-in-command and they captain. It's going to be a total of fifteen people and every one of them are going to die. And all their bodies I want laid out in the streets of Brooklyn. This is going to be a message like never before."

***

You had every family from the five boroughs at Symone's funeral. It was held on Albany Ave. at her family church. Symone's casket was covered with flowers of red, white, yellow and pink roses. You had the FBI there taking pictures of everyone. Jamila looked at everyone there before she stood up and walked to the mic to talk.

Saynomore

"You know, I look at my little sister laying here in this casket and the only thing I can think about is the first day she came into my life. She has always been a woman of her word. She has always been loyal. She is loved and will be missed. I love you, beautiful, kisses and hugs until we meet again, baby girl."

The funeral was two hours long; everyone was at Symone's burial. The heads of all five families came to talk to Jamila.

"Jamila, we came to pay our respects to you and your family. We are sorry for your loss. If there is anything we can do for you, we are here for you, Queen Don."

"Thank you, Mr. Lenacci, I'm glad you all are here. Tomorrow night I would like for all five families to get together. I'm giving my sister's family to my baby sister and I want to do it the right way with the five families and two witnesses from each family to be there."

"Jamila, on the blood of our oaths we will all be there. What time?"

"Nine p.m. at the old waste plant."

Everyone nodded and hugged and kissed Jamila on the cheek before walking away. Jamila walked back to her limo where Masi and Pistol were waiting for her.

"Did ya find our mystery man yet?" asked Jamila.

"Yea, we did. We have him tied up and waiting on you now to show up."

"Okay, Masi. Pistol, have Victorious and Iceman get with Muscle and have him bring them to the waste plant now."

"Yes, Ms. LaCross."

***

Perk G sat down looking at Carson Praise in the chair bleeding from the beating they been giving him all night. His hands were tied behind his back, and he had nothing on.

Perk G lit up a blunt and was smoking it when Jamila walked into the warehouse with Masi and Pistol right behind her. Jamila walked up to Carson Praise and looked into his eyes. "You killed my little sister. You cost your whole family they lives when you did that. You walked into the devil's playground and motherfucker, I'm the devil."

Jamila walked to Perk G.

"Where is his family at?"

"It was just him. He had no ID, just the one picture of Symone in his house," said Perk G.

"I'll find his family. I have my ways."

Within two minutes Victorious walked in the warehouse. She walked up to Jamila and gave her a hug.

"Beautiful," said Jamila, "let me introduce you to the man who killed our sister."

Victorious looked at him. "How are we going to kill him?"

"In the worst way. Masi, hand me the bat."

Masi went and handed Jamila the bat.

"Beautiful."

"Yes," replied Victorious.

"Go handle your business."

Victorious walked up to him.

"I hate you, motherfucker."

"Join the club," said Carson Praise.

Victorious swung the bat, smacking him in the face. His body hit the ground along with the chair he was tied to. All you heard was Victorious screaming as she beat him over and over. Jamila looked at Perk G and nodded. He got up with the crowbar he had in his hand. Victorious took two steps back and looked at Perk G.

"If I could, I would fucking kill you, but she told me I can't. But motherfucker, you are going to wish you was dead."

Perk G took the crowbar and slammed it as hard as he could to his ribcage over and over again then smacked him in the face, breaking his teeth out. "Perk G!" Jamila called him.

"Iceman, put him on the chains. Pistol, help hang him up. Muscle, go get me an ax. I want this motherfucker to know true pain. Masi, bring me a razor!" said Jamila.

Saynomore

Victorious watched as they hung his body on the chains from the ceiling. Jamila walked up to him and took the razor and cut a line down his chest.

"Uughh!"

"Does that hurt, motherfucker?" asked Jamila. "No, nigga, you ripped my fucking heart out my chest. I fucking hate you!" said Jamila.

Jamila took the razor and sliced his face open.

"Victorious, grab the metal cup and fill it up with acid and bring it to me."

Jamila threw the acid on his face. "Uuhhgg, uuhhgg."

"Go refill it now."

She then threw it on his chest; his body was shaking out of control.

"Katrina, my sister stamped you, right?" asked Jamila.

"Yes, she did."

"Come here."

Jamila looked at her and handed her the razor.

"Cut his throat from ear to ear."

Katrina placed the razor to his neck and cut his throat open. Blood covered her hand as she took his life.

"Wrap him up. He's going to lay with the rest of the families tomorrow night. Muscle, Masi, get it done. Victorious, come on, we are leaving, we have to get ready for tomorrow night," said Jamila.

Chapter Fifty-Two

Jamila looked out the window as the cars were pulling up one by one. She and Victorious were waiting for everyone to come inside the office room to sit at the round table. Jamila watched everyone come into the office one by one. She walked up to them all and shook their hands and gave them a kiss on the cheek.

"First, I would like to thank you all for coming to this meeting tonight. And I also want to thank all of you for your support these last few days. For everyone here who does not know, this is my sister Victorious. She will be taking over the Rose family as the head don. Victorious, there are five families. Each family has a borough they run. You will now be controlling Brooklyn. Let me introduce you to the families by name. From right to left you have the Gambino family, the Scott family, the Landon family, the Lenacci family and you know the LaCross family and the Teliono family. And now you have the Rose family. They cannot do any dealings outside of Brooklyn. Is there any question for Victorious Rose?" said Jamila to the families.

"I have one question."

"The table is yours, Mr. Scott."

"Should we expect retaliation for your sister's murder?"

"I do not know who killed her, but we are going to let the dead rest in peace. Again no one is bigger than the mob, no one. And the things that Rose was doing were out of control and her fate caught up with her in the end."

Iceman watched from a hole in the wall along with Pistol, Tasha, Muscle, Masi and Perk G. Everyone stood up. Jamila held Victorious' hand as she took two steps back. Mr. Scott looked in Jamila's eyes, but before he could let out a word bullets were rattling through the wall, hitting everyone at the table and those who were standing up. Victorious had never seen a massacre like this before. She watched as bodies hit the table and rolled on the floor. People was coughing up blood then the gunshots just stopped, and the side door opened up. Jamila walked up to Masi and Pistol.

"Give all of them a head shot. I want two bullets in each of their heads."

Jamila watched as they did what she told them to do. Not one person made it out of there alive.

"Jamila, do you think that this is going to come back on us?"

"No, it was an unsanctioned hit on the Rose family. What happened here is justified. Put the bodies in the van and place them where I told you to, Masi, in Brooklyn under the picture of Rose that was painted on the wall in Brooklyn. Put a sign on one of the necks that says, *Street justice is the best justice. You can sleep in peace now, Rose, we will forever love you.*"

Chapter Fifty-Three

"Excuse me, Special Agent Carter, Agent Brooks, you might want to come see this." Special Agent Carter and Agent Brooks looked at each other and followed the agent into the break room, where you had twenty other agents watching the news.

"Brooks, are you seeing this shit?"

"I see it, sir, but I can't believe what I'm seeing." Under the picture that was painted of Symone Rose there were flowers, cards, stuffed teddy bears and sixteen dead Italians. The news reporter read the sign that was around the neck of one of the Italians: *Street justice is the best justice! You can sleep in peace now, Rose, we will forever love you.*

"Brooks, we need to get down there now!" Special Agent Carter said as he rushed out the break room to his car with Agent Brooks right behind him.

***

Mr. Savato was playing pool as the news was on the TV in the pool hall.

"Pete, come see this."

"What I tell you, Pete, dead—all of them."

"This is what happens when you have an unsanctioned hit"

"Damn, Mr. Savato, she really stuck it to them."

"Turn this up. I can't hear what they are saying," Mr. Savato said. Once the volume was turned up, the voice of the reporter became really audible.

'Five mafia families all hit at one time. New York City has never witnessed anything like this in the history of New York. All men have multiple gunshots to the upper body and two gun shots to the back of the head. This is a deadly message to somebody. The one question is, do this have anything to do with Symone Rose's assassination?'

"This is why I said keep the guys out of New York City, Pete, the FEDs is gone to be all over this, mark my words, Pete. Now come on, let's have a drink to them all."

Saynomore

***

Jamila and Victorious placed flowers down at Symone's head stone. Jamila had Symone laid to rest next to their father's grave.

"You okay, beautiful?"

"Yea, I am."

"Victorious I want you to always remember Symone is with us in spirit. You have a big role to play now and your family needs you to step up. Remember, never show no signs of weakness."

"I won't."

Jamila hugged Victorious and kissed her forehead.

"Come on, let's go get something to eat, beautiful."

When they turned around they saw Detective Mayfield and another Detective standing there watching them.

"Ms. LaCross, I'm sorry for your loss, but I need to know, is this over now?"

"Thank you, Detective Mayfield, but I do not know what you are talking about. I'm here to pay my respect to my sister, that's all."

"Sure you are, Ms. LaCross, and who may you be?" Detective Mayfield looked at Victorious.

Jamila looked at both detectives.

"She nobody. Now if you would excuse me, Detective Mayfield."

Jamila walked back to her limo where Masi and Pistol were waiting for her at.

"What you think of that, Detective Mayfield?"

"In time we will have a name to go with the face. One thing I know—can't nobody hide in the shadow of the mob and what they try to hide in the dark always come to the light."

The End

Lock Down Publications and Ca$h Presents assisted publishing packages.

BASIC PACKAGE $499
Editing
Cover Design
Formatting

UPGRADED PACKAGE $800
Typing
Editing
Cover Design
Formatting

ADVANCE PACKAGE $1,200
Typing
Editing
Cover Design
Formatting
Copyright registration
Proofreading
Upload book to Amazon

LDP SUPREME PACKAGE $1,500
Typing
Editing
Cover Design
Formatting
Copyright registration
Proofreading
Set up Amazon account
Upload book to Amazon
Advertise on LDP Amazon and Facebook page

Saynomore

***Other services available upon request. Additional charges may apply
Lock Down Publications
P.O. Box 944
Stockbridge, GA 30281-9998
Phone # 470 303-9761

Submission Guideline

Submit the first three chapters of your completed manuscript to ldpsubmissions@gmail.com, subject line: Your book's title. The manuscript must be in a .doc file and sent as an attachment. Document should be in Times New Roman, double spaced and in size 12 font. Also, provide your synopsis and full contact information. If sending multiple submissions, they must each be in a separate email.

Have a story but no way to send it electronically? You can still submit to LDP/Ca$h Presents. Send in the first three chapters, written or typed, of your completed manuscript to:

**LDP: Submissions Dept
Po Box 944
Stockbridge, Ga 30281**

DO NOT send original manuscript. Must be a duplicate.

Provide your synopsis and a cover letter containing your full contact information.

Thanks for considering LDP and Ca$h Presents.

Saynomore

NEW RELEASES

VICIOIUS LOYALTY 2 by KINGPEN
THE STREETS WILL NEVER CLOSE 3 by K'AJJI
THE MURDER QUEENS by MICHAEL GALLON
THE BIRTHN OF A GANGSTA by DELMONT PLAYER
MOB TIES 6 by SAYNOMORE

Mob Ties 6

Coming Soon from Lock Down Publications/Ca$h Presents

BLOOD OF A BOSS **VI**

SHADOWS OF THE GAME II

TRAP BASTARD II

By **Askari**

LOYAL TO THE GAME **IV**

By **T.J. & Jelissa**

IF TRUE SAVAGE **VIII**

MIDNIGHT CARTEL IV

DOPE BOY MAGIC IV

CITY OF KINGZ III

NIGHTMARE ON SILENT AVE II

THE PLUG OF LIL MEXICO II

By **Chris Green**

BLAST FOR ME **III**

A SAVAGE DOPEBOY III

CUTTHROAT MAFIA III

DUFFLE BAG CARTEL VII

HEARTLESS GOON VI

By **Ghost**

A HUSTLER'S DECEIT III

KILL ZONE II

BAE BELONGS TO ME III

By **Aryanna**

KING OF THE TRAP III

By **T.J. Edwards**

GORILLAZ IN THE BAY V

3X KRAZY III

STRAIGHT BEAST MODE II

De'Kari

Saynomore

KINGPIN KILLAZ IV
STREET KINGS III
PAID IN BLOOD III
CARTEL KILLAZ IV
DOPE GODS III
Hood Rich
SINS OF A HUSTLA II
ASAD
RICH $AVAGE II
By Martell Troublesome Bolden
YAYO V
Bred In The Game 2
S. Allen
CREAM III
THE STREETS WILL TALK II
By Yolanda Moore
SON OF A DOPE FIEND III
HEAVEN GOT A GHETTO II
By Renta
LOYALTY AIN'T PROMISED III
By Keith Williams
I'M NOTHING WITHOUT HIS LOVE II
SINS OF A THUG II
TO THE THUG I LOVED BEFORE II
IN A HUSTLER I TRUST II
By Monet Dragun
QUIET MONEY IV
EXTENDED CLIP III
THUG LIFE IV
By **Trai'Quan**

THE STREETS MADE ME IV
By **Larry D. Wright**
IF YOU CROSS ME ONCE II
By **Anthony Fields**
THE STREETS WILL NEVER CLOSE IV
By **K'ajji**
HARD AND RUTHLESS III
KILLA KOUNTY III
By Khufu
MONEY GAME III
By Smoove Dolla
JACK BOYS VS DOPE BOYS II
A GANGSTA'S QUR'AN V
COKE GIRLZ II
By Romell Tukes
MURDA WAS THE CASE II
Elijah R. Freeman
THE STREETS NEVER LET GO II
By Robert Baptiste
AN UNFORESEEN LOVE III
By **Meesha**
KING OF THE TRENCHES III
by **GHOST & TRANAY ADAMS**

MONEY MAFIA II
LOYAL TO THE SOIL III
By **Jibril Williams**
QUEEN OF THE ZOO II
By **Black Migo**
THE BRICK MAN IV
By King Rio

Saynomore

VICIOUS LOYALTY III
By Kingpen
A GANGSTA'S PAIN II
By J-Blunt
CONFESSIONS OF A JACKBOY III
By Nicholas Lock
GRIMEY WAYS II
By Ray Vinci
KING KILLA II
By Vincent "Vitto" Holloway
BETRAYAL OF A THUG II
By Fre$h
THE MURDER QUEENS II
By Michael Gallon
THE BIRTH OF A GANGSTA II
By Delmont Player

Available Now

RESTRAINING ORDER **I & II**
By **CA$H & Coffee**
LOVE KNOWS NO BOUNDARIES **I II & III**
By **Coffee**
RAISED AS A GOON I, II, III & IV
BRED BY THE SLUMS I, II, III
BLAST FOR ME I & II
ROTTEN TO THE CORE I II III

Mob Ties 6

A BRONX TALE I, II, III
DUFFLE BAG CARTEL I II III IV V VI
HEARTLESS GOON I II III IV V
A SAVAGE DOPEBOY I II
DRUG LORDS I II III
CUTTHROAT MAFIA I II
KING OF THE TRENCHES
By **Ghost**
LAY IT DOWN **I & II**
LAST OF A DYING BREED I II
BLOOD STAINS OF A SHOTTA I & II III
By **Jamaica**
LOYAL TO THE GAME I II III
LIFE OF SIN I, II III
By **TJ & Jelissa**
BLOODY COMMAS I & II
SKI MASK CARTEL I II & III
KING OF NEW YORK I II,III IV V
RISE TO POWER I II III
COKE KINGS I II III IV V
BORN HEARTLESS I II III IV
KING OF THE TRAP I II
By **T.J. Edwards**
IF LOVING HIM IS WRONG…I & II
LOVE ME EVEN WHEN IT HURTS I II III
By **Jelissa**
WHEN THE STREETS CLAP BACK I & II III
THE HEART OF A SAVAGE I II III
MONEY MAFIA
LOYAL TO THE SOIL I II

Saynomore

By **Jibril Williams**
A DISTINGUISHED THUG STOLE MY HEART I II & III
LOVE SHOULDN'T HURT I II III IV
RENEGADE BOYS I II III IV
PAID IN KARMA I II III
SAVAGE STORMS I II III
AN UNFORESEEN LOVE I II

By **Meesha**
A GANGSTER'S CODE I &, II III
A GANGSTER'S SYN I II III
THE SAVAGE LIFE I II III
CHAINED TO THE STREETS I II III
BLOOD ON THE MONEY I II III
A GANGSTA'S PAIN

By **J-Blunt**
PUSH IT TO THE LIMIT

By **Bre' Hayes**
BLOOD OF A BOSS **I, II, III, IV, V**
SHADOWS OF THE GAME
TRAP BASTARD

By **Askari**
THE STREETS BLEED MURDER **I, II & III**
THE HEART OF A GANGSTA I II& III

By **Jerry Jackson**
CUM FOR ME I II III IV V VI VII VIII

An **LDP Erotica Collaboration**
BRIDE OF A HUSTLA **I II & II**
THE FETTI GIRLS **I, II& III**
CORRUPTED BY A GANGSTA I, II III, IV
BLINDED BY HIS LOVE

Mob Ties 6

THE PRICE YOU PAY FOR LOVE I, II ,III
DOPE GIRL MAGIC I II III
By **Destiny Skai**
WHEN A GOOD GIRL GOES BAD
By **Adrienne**
THE COST OF LOYALTY I II III
By **Kweli**
A GANGSTER'S REVENGE **I II III & IV**
THE BOSS MAN'S DAUGHTERS I II III IV V
A SAVAGE LOVE **I & II**
BAE BELONGS TO ME I II
A HUSTLER'S DECEIT I, II, III
WHAT BAD BITCHES DO I, II, III
SOUL OF A MONSTER I II III
KILL ZONE
A DOPE BOY'S QUEEN I II III
By **Aryanna**
A KINGPIN'S AMBITON
A KINGPIN'S AMBITION **II**
I MURDER FOR THE DOUGH
By **Ambitious**
TRUE SAVAGE I II III IV V VI VII
DOPE BOY MAGIC I, II, III
MIDNIGHT CARTEL I II III
CITY OF KINGZ I II
NIGHTMARE ON SILENT AVE
THE PLUG OF LIL MEXICO II

By **Chris Green**
A DOPEBOY'S PRAYER

Saynomore

By **Eddie "Wolf" Lee**
THE KING CARTEL **I, II & III**
By **Frank Gresham**
THESE NIGGAS AIN'T LOYAL **I, II & III**
By **Nikki Tee**
GANGSTA SHYT **I II &III**
By **CATO**
THE ULTIMATE BETRAYAL
By **Phoenix**
BOSS'N UP **I , II & III**
By **Royal Nicole**
I LOVE YOU TO DEATH
By **Destiny J**
I RIDE FOR MY HITTA
I STILL RIDE FOR MY HITTA
By **Misty Holt**
LOVE & CHASIN' PAPER
By **Qay Crockett**
TO DIE IN VAIN
SINS OF A HUSTLA
By **ASAD**
BROOKLYN HUSTLAZ
By **Boogsy Morina**
BROOKLYN ON LOCK I & II
By **Sonovia**
GANGSTA CITY
By **Teddy Duke**
A DRUG KING AND HIS DIAMOND I & II III
A DOPEMAN'S RICHES
HER MAN, MINE'S TOO I, II

Mob Ties 6

CASH MONEY HO'S
THE WIFEY I USED TO BE I II
By Nicole Goosby
TRAPHOUSE KING **I II & III**
KINGPIN KILLAZ I II III
STREET KINGS I II
PAID IN BLOOD **I II**
CARTEL KILLAZ I II III
DOPE GODS I II
By **Hood Rich**
LIPSTICK KILLAH **I, II, III**
CRIME OF PASSION I II & III
FRIEND OR FOE I II III
By **Mimi**
STEADY MOBBN' **I, II, III**
THE STREETS STAINED MY SOUL I II III
By **Marcellus Allen**
WHO SHOT YA **I, II, III**
SON OF A DOPE FIEND I II
HEAVEN GOT A GHETTO
Renta
GORILLAZ IN THE BAY **I II III IV**
TEARS OF A GANGSTA I II
3X KRAZY I II
STRAIGHT BEAST MODE
DE'KARI
TRIGGADALE I II III
MURDAROBER WAS THE CASE
Elijah R. Freeman
GOD BLESS THE TRAPPERS I, II, III

Saynomore

THESE SCANDALOUS STREETS I, II, III
FEAR MY GANGSTA I, II, III IV, V
THESE STREETS DON'T LOVE NOBODY I, II
BURY ME A G I, II, III, IV, V
A GANGSTA'S EMPIRE I, II, III, IV
THE DOPEMAN'S BODYGAURD I II
THE REALEST KILLAZ I II III
THE LAST OF THE OGS I II III
Tranay Adams
THE STREETS ARE CALLING
Duquie Wilson
MARRIED TO A BOSS I II III
By Destiny Skai & Chris Green
KINGZ OF THE GAME I II III IV V VI
Playa Ray
SLAUGHTER GANG I II III
RUTHLESS HEART I II III
By Willie Slaughter
FUK SHYT
By Blakk Diamond
DON'T F#CK WITH MY HEART I II
By Linnea
ADDICTED TO THE DRAMA I II III
IN THE ARM OF HIS BOSS II
By Jamila
YAYO I II III IV
A SHOOTER'S AMBITION I II
BRED IN THE GAME
By S. Allen
TRAP GOD I II III

Mob Ties 6

RICH $AVAGE
MONEY IN THE GRAVE I II III
By Martell Troublesome Bolden
FOREVER GANGSTA
GLOCKS ON SATIN SHEETS I II
By Adrian Dulan
TOE TAGZ I II III IV
LEVELS TO THIS SHYT I II
By Ah'Million
KINGPIN DREAMS I II III
By Paper Boi Rari
CONFESSIONS OF A GANGSTA I II III IV
CONFESSIONS OF A JACKBOY I II
By Nicholas Lock
I'M NOTHING WITHOUT HIS LOVE
SINS OF A THUG
TO THE THUG I LOVED BEFORE
A GANGSTA SAVED XMAS
IN A HUSTLER I TRUST
By Monet Dragun
CAUGHT UP IN THE LIFE I II III
THE STREETS NEVER LET GO
By Robert Baptiste
NEW TO THE GAME I II III
MONEY, MURDER & MEMORIES I II III
By **Malik D. Rice**
LIFE OF A SAVAGE I II III
A GANGSTA'S QUR'AN I II III IV
MURDA SEASON I II III
GANGLAND CARTEL I II III

Saynomore

CHI'RAQ GANGSTAS I II III
KILLERS ON ELM STREET I II III
JACK BOYZ N DA BRONX I II III
A DOPEBOY'S DREAM I II III
JACK BOYS VS DOPE BOYS
COKE GIRLZ
By Romell Tukes
LOYALTY AIN'T PROMISED I II
By Keith Williams
QUIET MONEY I II III
THUG LIFE I II III
EXTENDED CLIP I II
By **Trai'Quan**
THE STREETS MADE ME I II III
By **Larry D. Wright**
THE ULTIMATE SACRIFICE I, II, III, IV, V, VI
KHADIFI
IF YOU CROSS ME ONCE
ANGEL I II
IN THE BLINK OF AN EYE
By **Anthony Fields**
THE LIFE OF A HOOD STAR
By Ca$h & Rashia Wilson
THE STREETS WILL NEVER CLOSE I II III
By K'ajji
CREAM I II
THE STREETS WILL TALK
By Yolanda Moore
NIGHTMARES OF A HUSTLA I II III
By King Dream

Mob Ties 6

CONCRETE KILLA I II

VICIOUS LOYALTY I II

By Kingpen

HARD AND RUTHLESS I II

MOB TOWN 251

THE BILLIONAIRE BENTLEYS I II III

By Von Diesel

GHOST MOB

Stilloan Robinson

MOB TIES I II III IV V VI

By SayNoMore

BODYMORE MURDERLAND I II III

THE BIRTH OF A GANGSTA

By Delmont Player

FOR THE LOVE OF A BOSS

By C. D. Blue

MOBBED UP I II III IV

THE BRICK MAN I II III

THE COCAINE PRINCESS I II III IV V

By King Rio

KILLA KOUNTY I II III

By Khufu

MONEY GAME I II

By Smoove Dolla

A GANGSTA'S KARMA I II

By FLAME

KING OF THE TRENCHES I II

by **GHOST & TRANAY ADAMS**

QUEEN OF THE ZOO

By **Black Migo**

Saynomore

GRIMEY WAYS
By Ray Vinci
XMAS WITH AN ATL SHOOTER
By Ca$h & Destiny Skai
KING KILLA
By Vincent "Vitto" Holloway
BETRAYAL OF A THUG
By Fre$h
THE MURDER QUEENS
By Michael Gallon

Mob Ties 6

BOOKS BY LDP'S CEO, CA$H

TRUST IN NO MAN
TRUST IN NO MAN 2
TRUST IN NO MAN 3
BONDED BY BLOOD
SHORTY GOT A THUG
THUGS CRY
THUGS CRY 2
THUGS CRY 3
TRUST NO BITCH
TRUST NO BITCH 2
TRUST NO BITCH 3
TIL MY CASKET DROPS
RESTRAINING ORDER
RESTRAINING ORDER 2
IN LOVE WITH A CONVICT
LIFE OF A HOOD STAR
XMAS WITH AN ATL SHOOTER

Saynomore